MT. SUMMER

Published in the United States by Out to Lunch Records: www.outtolunchrecords.com. If you wish to use or reproduce all or part of this book for any means, please let the author and publisher know.

ISBN 978-0-578-30488-5
Library of Congress Control Number: 2021920939

Cover Design by John Shields

First paperback edition.

MOUNT SUMMER

STORIES BY TRAVIS DAHLKE

ILLUSTRATED BY JOHN SHIELDS

SOUNDTRACK BY FiFac (JEFF DRAGAN)

OUT TO LUNCH RECORDS
MA/FL/ES

The MOUNT SUMMER original soundtrack is available at fifac.bandcamp.com.

Visit outtolunchrecords.com for information on additional download codes.

I asked, where do tourists go when they die? You told me they go to *Tourist Heaven*.

WHAT IS A WOLF TREE

On the hottest afternoon of September, in the deepest part of the forest, there's this tree that appears to have lived its entire life dead. Where a thick branch used to be, there's a cavity filled in with: BIC lighters, a vial containing the blood of a country music star, Advil, unopened mail, a pocketknife with a faux-wood grip and grandmother models cut from last fall's Eddie Bauer catalog.

Seven hundred thousand years earlier, the wilderness of New England had been leveled to make dairy barns. Its destroyers stood at the lip of their new habitat and felt cured. No matter which way they craned their sunburned necks, they were faced with a pasture that repeated itself in either baby shit green or regular green. The destroyers liked how everything was the same. They liked how artists painted pictures of this. The artists liked when songs were made up about their paintings, only for new artists to create new paintings based on their songs. When the destroyers married one another, their pastures were played back to them on harps and drums, and that just made everyone a little happier.

But there was more forest to undo and for each acre of wood turned into another structure, a few trees were left to provide shade for cattle. As the destroyers raised empty hands to their mouths, they would play God, using their axes for *mana, mike; Barcelona, mona, strike!* This decided which elms, black maples, and oaks would survive. The downed trees went into stoves. From chimneys across the mega-pasture came dozens of smoke tubes, like veins carrying soot toward an invisible artery. The surviving trees watched this and didn't complain. All the violence they saw they ate, and they never got hungry. At night by their fires, the destroyers consoled one another with how nice it was of them to leave a souvenir of what the land originally resembled.

Stones in the ground were replaced with seeds to grow: rye, strawberries, barley, squash, hops, corn, lentils. The destroyers preferred to use the word "impregnate" when they tilled, or while they watched rain turn from a sprinkle to sheets upon the upturned earth. The rocks spit up by the ground were piled to fill in property lines. Snow glued them into walls. These stone walls were the hiding place for: dandruff, bar soap made from grapefruit, coins carrying trace amounts of cocaine, rust freckled scissors, one thimble, ornament-eyed sea serpents that had escaped from the forests. During the winter everyone locked their doors and didn't come out for exactly five months. The wolf trees watched the green leave their landscapes. The destroyers burned their wood and called the snow a blanket.

When the pastures thawed, the destroyers ambled outside to stretch their limbs. They worked under the sun and were made partially deaf by: grasshoppers, bees. As the sun drew closer, the bees roared louder. New bees that came across on European ships roared back while building great planets oozing with liquid sugar. After there were enough walls, it was the sea serpents that took care of the noise.

The offspring of the destroyers married one another. Daffodils, crocus and marigolds were used as creative solutions for tiaras. There were more houses to build with more stoves. Each new house put a woolly, hot feeling in their collective gut. When they ran out of land to turn, the destroyers and the children of the destroyers whet their appetites by turning their unmarried into witches. *Look at their gross hats*, the destroyers said. *Those are for keeping out the Lord's sun. Look at their claws. Those are for digging nests in our seabeds.*

It was the wolf trees, with their strong backs, the destroyers used for executions. The witches came apart in papyrus vines. Their discharge, black and butter-like, fed the soil, and the soil, in turn, acquired a taste for one-piece bathing suits. It refused anything else. The destroyers liked destroying their witches during thunderstorms because the light was more dramatic. All the boots, clothing, and turquoise jewelry was cremated to make rainbow sand art. No matter what season it was, the destroyers built fires. Fires just made everyone feel a little better.

After a hundred million weddings, the feeling of being cured had waned so gradually the destroyers barely noticed, and as pollen sleepwalked down from the trees, so did something that made them all very sick. The stone walls were dismantled to make gravestones. Lichen preferred to grow in the inscriptions and was especially partial toward the number eight.

With the pastures left to grow wild, the wolf trees raised themselves. Young saplings and shrubs returned. They did their best to insulate their ancestors from the weather but often its violence was too much to bear and the trees couldn't keep from remembering, and so parts of them died and bugs made homes in these parts. Birds and small mammals fed on the bugs and then shit nourishment into the wolf trees' soil in an effort to keep them alive for longer. *They're all we have left of how it used to be*, the animals said. *We can't let them go just yet.*

In summary, the wolf tree was once surrounded by wolf trees, until it was surrounded by pasture until it was surrounded again by forest. The wolf tree is both taller and older than everything else in the forest. The air slurs around its mouth. It has an octopus for a shadow that freaks you out, so you try and see if you can remember how to get home.

WOLF MALLS

A wolf mall is pretty similar to a wolf tree. They are the result of clear-cutting Main Street, whose bones and hair and meat are used to build the much better wolf mall. When smaller predators try to stand up to it, the wolf mall will bare the yellow crud on its rearmost fangs and swallow them whole. Everything in the wolf mall is glass to nourish potted ferns, for children to bury their Hot Wheels in when no one is looking. The wolf mall is a transient place that comes alive in certain seasons, going in and out of hibernation.

You were created by the wolf mall. Its 99 Restaurant with strong daiquiris abetted in unbuckling khakis in its furthest parking spaces. It was there when your spirit was formed to Dolly Parton crackling across the radio. You were raised by the wolf mall. Your parents achieved credit at a store that sold bibs and onesies with cute quotes on them like *I Like Big Naps and I Cannot Lie* and *I'm Not Crying I'm Ordering Dinner.* Hard plastic horse snouts from the carousel filled your nightmares before you could remember your nightmares. You balanced on Santa's good knee and returned to get your upper cartilage pierced at Claire's and then Hot Topic for the jewelry. The person piercing you didn't even check your fake ID. You complimented the Tasmanian Devil tattoo on her throat. She was too busy falling in love with the redneck security guards who strolled by on their thick blue legs.

Using the money your dad placed in an old graduation card, you bought your mom a pre-wrapped gift basket with bath salts and lavender essential oil from the Gifts4theDeservingMom display. Your parents said you'd be doomed as a witch if you chose not to marry that nice Alex, who gave you burned CDs and gift cards from Waldenbooks. The mixes always culminated in a slow jam. You imagined your wedding guests wincing at the glitchy blips cutting up what Alex downloaded off LimeWire. In the perfumed fog of the arcade, your best friend Joshua warned you Alex was a kleptomaniac and that his gift cards were duds. He said this while blasting pixel bullets at pixel witches and you yearned for the beautiful, most greenest-haired ones to visit you at night in dreams. They never did, because when the mall closed, the security guards stole the witches from where they slept in their arcade cabinets to crucify them below terrarium glass. This was part of a ritual.

Now you're older and have money you don't know what to do with, so you go to the mall and leave it there. Your former best friend, Joshua, crushes his eye socket in a skeet shooting accident. It's in the newspaper. Eventually you're so old that every day feels like that one time you caught the flu except this is forever. You arrive right when the mall opens, just to walk it. You've been brought there in a white van. You point to the ruins where the 99 Restaurant once stood and say, *boy if only that cinder could talk.* The receiving bay is the underbelly of the mall but you think maybe the mall itself is becoming an underbelly. Here are broken arcade games. You use the word "defeated" to explain them and wipe away the dust from Witch Slayer II. You give a reassuring pat to Area 51, as well as the fortune teller game which doesn't have a name. *ALL the parts of ur future are lying in wait. Assembly required,* is burned into the screen.

At some point, it's just spirits roaming the palms and chlorine fountains. They think they're on vacation. The flu follows the spirit. Your body feeds on salted soda and in turn, the mall feeds on you, but it isn't enough. You try to tell people the mall was a wonderful place in its time. You try to tell people about the miniature rusted Camaro swallowed by the soil of the palm tree yet there's no one to listen.

The anchor store closes. It takes any loitering nutrients with it. There's something about the mall's shell that makes you nervous. The Wikipedia entry for seashell says *the shells are empty because the animal has died and the soft parts have been eaten by another animal or have decomposed.* Behind pulled down shutters are: paper towels, wire racks, someone's final mop trails, one soda cup. The Auntie Anne's/Filene's perfume department smell never goes away. Even when the structures have been demolished and new ones are built, you can still tell.

WOLF BEACHES

Wolf beaches are much harder to define.

WHEN YOU DIE IN RHODE ISLAND, YOU DIE IN REAL LIFE

Joanne that looks deciduous, I say, lying about her brunch leftovers. Delicious I mean. Thank you it's from The Oyster House where I went with Marty this weekend. She's using our microwave to warm it up. My pen won't reach the carbon copy no matter how hard I force it. The stack is so thin because no one puts their kids in dance class during the summer.

I melted the fish she says. It's ooze now, and I gag when she says this. They get all their herring from Chatham, I swear to God they have the best brunch outside of the city. Goddamnit, I forgot we have to return the Rug Doctor, let's do that, Joanne says.

This is a dead pen, I say, and I hate that Stop & Shop. It's so dirty.

You know I heard a guy was begging Katheryn Pelletier for money there and followed her outside to her car? I lock my doors in that part of town. Everyone does. But it was the only place that had an actual steam cleaner can you believe that? She plays with the angle of a fan which creaks at her touch like it's very sick. Most parents right now are showing their children Barcelona or how to kayak in glacial runoff.

Our carpets are cleaned twice a year. Joanne uses an extension cord to plug the machine in. Those eggs are sitting strange with me. She rigs it at the tack strip. Paul Feinstein and his daughter are early for their class. Hi Amelia, I say, did you have fun in Brussels. Yes, she says.

I open the window and reposition the fan. Joanne is throwing the heavy cord of the steamer around. She flips it on and she is making a high-pitched sound. What is that, she says. I turn to see a chocolaty pool crawling out from the canister. It's reflected in each mirror. Paul Feinstein swoops his daughter up, covering her face with his palm.

It's just gushing out nonstop. Turn it off I tell her, and she does not remember how she turned it on. She yanks the cord out of the wall but the pool is gaining territory on the hardwood planks, seeping into each gap. The door opens and Lucy Vasserbelt walks in with her mom but her mom is on the phone and she walks right through it. Mrs. Vasserbelt I say, Mrs. Vasserbelt please stop. She is tracking it onto the carpet with her sandals and has just started to notice something is wrong.

It stops growing, having reached its final form as a slice off the surface of a very deep and awful pond. Mrs. Vasserbelt looks terrified of her own footprints.

Is it blood? I say. Joanne is still yelling and burping. All at once we recognize a place we thought was very far away.

Yes, I think it is, she says. All of it.

MOUNT SUMMER

Nine times out of twelve the new guy tries to show off and does irreversible damage to their whole ass spine. That's a guaranteed call-out followed by three months of disability, which then overlaps into their trial period. Next thing you know, they've died from acute Stouffer's poisoning. That's all it takes to die from eating pure Stouffer's. Three months.

But it was so sunny that day that all I could think about was Patricia Chanstein's mustardy-colored hair. I thought about how it actually tasted like mustard when it got in your mouth. I thought about it, smoothing out air pockets in the decal I applied to the side of our van. At some point, my new partner Del would ask about Patricia because the first day in the van means horseshitting about old girlfriends. This creates a comfort barrier that only then allows us to do our job properly.

There was nothing about this Del I trusted because he was fresh out of the Felon Reentry & Transition program. Who knows what grisly crime landed him there in the first place? He looked like an inmate too, right down to how fast he ate powdered donuts, and the inked manatee fighting an eel on the back of his pasty ass shaved head where he had an apparatus stapled to his skull. Goggle-style sunglasses made red marks in his neck rolls, on the largest of which was printed the name *Mallory Lee.*

He stood still as boards and always spoke as if talking to a dangerous animal he was trying to calm down. I figured he must've killed at least three people. There was no doubt in my mind he would forgo a brace and pull something, fast-tracking himself to the glorious neon of Disability City.

We hit Cumby's first to get fucked up on lattes, extra French vanilla and cinnamon, extra non-dairy creamer, extra straws, extra whipped cream. I watched Del dump exactly seven packets of Splenda in his. Two X-Jumbo lattes were enough to get smiles on us for the photo of our new van decal requested by our boss. The caffeine momentarily made my brain feel like

Patricia was still super in love with me. It made me want to send her a message but then it would look like I wasn't busy, which I was.

The phone our company provided us was a burner Motorola that took grainy postal stamps for photos. Our van's decal portrayed a caricature of someone who was not our boss, using small arms from a small body to juggle a stack of boxes. The decal boiled with air pockets that in my opinion gave a certain texture. "Sets us apart from the big guys," I told Del.

"If you say so."

Our job was clear cut—an estate where the owner hadn't exactly died, but was aged in place by his kids somewhere off the shore. His youngest heir was there to give us directions with a perfect haircut in a see-through shirt tucked into his cowboy boots. He shook my hand gently but not Del's and said his name was McCade. He didn't give great directions because he was missing work and why should he be the one who has to deal with the movers.

The house was cavernous somehow even on the outside, uniformed by peeling paint as if its rotten panels were shaking off a sunburn. It sat at the end of a long dirt driveway on what must've been at least eleven acres.

Del didn't like the look of the house. Post-WWII. Bad stuff in there. "Look at the winders." (He said windows like winders.) "They're black, can't even see into them, like they're painted. You can just tell how bad the back of your throat will burn being in there for even a second. Nothing good's in there. Shaun II isn't paying us enough."

On the lawn was a single dumpster. The phone number stenciled in spray paint was familiar. We fought through the hornets and dead flower smells overflowing from it. The heirs picked through everything in the main house, leaving us only bulky furniture and a full attic without a light bulb, so it was a good thing we came in the morning on such a shiny day. In the back of the parlor (this house had a parlor), a piano was tagged with electric tape for a bonfire the heir's own heirs were planning. Most of the attic was packed away in boxes, marked in what I'd guess was French. Del did not wager a guess as to what language it was.

We moved out a Victorian fainting couch, a chest of drawers, several ivory lamps, a painting of a barn by a beach framed in gold foil that jangled when we shook it, a portrait of a country singer on velvet, a box of spoken word records, a mountain bike, and an old-fashioned Pepsi ad, in addition to a whole lot of boxes that were sealed shut with duct tape. Any open boxes we were instructed not to touch.

McCade was outside smoking by his old swing set looking real lost-like. The swing set was swarmed by bees. It was getting cold outside and he had put a sweatshirt on over his dress shirt.

"That's it," I said.

McCade stomped out his cig as if I were his dad catching him from a long time ago. He offered to steal us some alcoholic seltzers from the party stash. "My kid won't mind," he said. The hornets moved on to the hummingbird feeder. Everyone leaves hummingbird feeders behind.

"Strange to see those fuckers so late in the season," McCade said.

We agreed, sipping from cans. We waited for him to sign our form while he made the final sweep upstairs. Landscapers were hauling leaves into the dumpster. Del nodded at them and they nodded back. I figured we were at least a half-hour ahead of schedule. Our drop-off spot was maybe an hour away, so we were doing good, though I had to piss real bad from the lattes.

"I'm going to take a piss," I told Del.

"Not here. He's going to be right back," Del said.

"He's cool, it's fine," I said.

McCade yelled from inside the house, "Hey, what's this? You're not done yet."

We followed him up into the attic, still holding our drinks like we weren't even on the clock.

"You didn't get it all out." He was starting another cigarette.

"Sir, we did," I told him.

McCade pointed toward the far end of the attic.

"Get that fuckin' head out of here," he said. At the receiving end of his ring finger was a pony or maybe a bigfoot head attached to the wall.

"No signature until that's gone," he said and snatched back our seltzers, tossing them half-full into a box where they turned the cardboard black.

"It's not a real animal, sir," I said.

"I don't care. You're not done until everything's out," McCade said. He stomped down the ladder.

We tried for a good fifteen minutes but the pony/bigfoot wouldn't come off. We took small breaks to catch our breath. I had never lost the baby weight after my son was born. "I used to be able to run eight miles in under an hour," I told Del. I positioned my legs wide and gave it a real solid pull, but it wouldn't budge.

"Try fuckin' harder," he said.

Del turned pink trying to separate the head from the wall. It was the most I'd seen him move. It was the most I'd seen anyone move, really. He kept stopping to clutch his left arm. Any minute I was ready to watch him reel backward and die. I'd have to smuggle him out in a tarp, sneak him into the van and drop his body into the Connecticut River down by the Dairy Queen where they go crabbing. His parole officer, secretly having an affair with him, would come for me.

On the fifteenth try of my wrenching on this pony/bigfoot head, I could feel my lower back pinch. Really pinch, like it was going to kill tomorrow and the month after, even though I was smart and wore a brace. I took a break to piss in the corner of the attic, while Del tried punching the wall around the head to loosen it.

"Go ahead, Del, you try again," I said. He pulled. Told me to stand back. "Wait, I have an idea." I went outside, making sure to avoid McCade, who was on his phone. He gave me a look as I passed. I returned from the van with a knife, a real serious-looking thing with notches that I had planned to use to whittle my kid a track baton with his name on it. I drove the knife in, wedging it behind the badge-shaped plank which allotted for some give. The seal broke.

Del's fists bulged out with veins and the pony/bigfoot finally tore away, knocking the three of us to the attic's floor. Years of mummified bat shit, dust, and soot erupted from behind the head all the way into my insides so that everything felt so dry that I convulsed in violent coughing. Insulation followed as snow, drifting to feather us and I realized it didn't have a smell. All the worst things don't have smells: carbon monoxide, marble, vodka in a Poland Spring bottle, stomach cancer mistaken for true love, Asbestos.

"Oh no."

Del looked to me with the horrible realization on his face. "Fuckin' no way, man."

In a panic we tried wiping the fibers off, sending them into the air. The asbestos floated back down. I covered all my face holes, but my palms were gloved in it. Insulation made from the thinnest fibers. Black glitter. Widow lint.

We forced coughs when the coughing stopped, feverishly trying to rub it away without rubbing it in. The heir was drinking in one of the swings as we left. We didn't wait for a tip or a signature or anything. We drove into an emerald forest, exerting the engine, kicking up sap puddles on the side of the road with every turn. Under one-half bar of reception, I sent Shaun Rice II the picture from this morning of us smiling by his decal, lattes engorging our heads. He received this with a thumbs-up emoji from whatever tropical island he was spending his vacation on.

"Hurry up, man," I told Del. "We gotta dump this load and get this junk the fuck off us."

We sped all the way to the next meeting spot. I thought about Patricia wearing her black leggings at my wake. Our kid in the folding chair next to her, refusing to talk. Yes, a vow of silence. Patricia would be watching the

Polaroids stapled to the photo collage. She'd be sucking back moments she took for granted, back into her throat where they would stay forever until she died heartbroken in the sleeping bag she laid over her mattress.

In the parking lot of a hiking trail, we found the second van, driven by a moon crater-faced kid in a black wig who helped us take inventory. Del pulled our vans ass to ass. We played it cool. Didn't mention how toxic we were. The kid gave us some weed, which at least calmed me down somewhat. He ripped the decal off our van and slapped on a magnet that said Stone Wall Office Supplies, in its former spot. The wig shook when he jumped back to take a picture. His company phone was nicer than ours. He got in our seats while we got in his. They were flaked leather and smelled like hot Sprite, probably from the Wendy's he left in the cup holder.

"$12,540 overall," I said, checking the invoice. *Not bad.* I said, "But fuck the rest of today, we got to get ourselves pure. I already feel like I have ten different cancers."

Del said he had it under control and that he beat skin cancer twice.

"Everyone beats skin cancer," I said. *Not everyone.* I thought of the pony/bigfoot. We drove in what felt like circles, losing precious time. I scanned for public fountains, car washes, gas stations with vacuums, anything.

"Over there. Gyms have showers," Del said, pointing to a plaza's Fitness Galaxy. We parked the van in a distant spot and jogged toward the gym through a crowd of people carrying grocery bags. There was barely anyone inside. A guy at the front desk was taking a credit card number from a girl wearing a sports bra underneath a winter jacket lined in fur.

"Whoa, whoa, hey." The guy started giving us shit, probably because we tried scanning our Cumby's cards and were standing in his Fitness Galaxy wearing canvas jumpsuits.

"But there's like zero people in here," I said to him. I couldn't read his nametag. An elderly man on a steeply-inclined treadmill glanced toward us before going back to his iPad.

"We could die," I whispered. "Level with us dude. This is an emergency."

"I'm calling the cops," he said, and we left.

Back in the van, Del remembered a gulch not far from the Fitness Galaxy we could wash the asbestos off in.

"My great-great-aunt ran a quarry there. Water's green as grass," he said.

The new van, which had way more horsepower, hurled us out from town onto a divided highway bordered by what looked like acres of tomato plants. I thought about Bart Simpson in overalls pulling the skin away from a tomato filled with tobacco. Season eleven would loop on the tiny television kept in the kitchen of the Alabamian Italian restaurant where I spent years scrubbing red sauce off steel. Patricia Chanstein was the waitress who smelt like vanilla bathroom spray and cantaloupe when she stomped by with her huge feet. Who would laugh at everything you said and who was so friendly with our customers. We fell in love to bleach on garlic salt. To ice machines churning black algae.

With spores burrowing into our skin, I told Del about Italian restaurants. I told him about the love of my damn ass life and how we began with a long engagement, followed by Patricia's dented ovaries that made us believe we couldn't get pregnant until the day she was three months deep with our son. Then I told Del about the apartment in Psalm Beach.

"We figured we nabbed that apartment cheap because the neighborhood had some drug problems and the whole complex was directly under airliner paths. The realtor promised us that ceramic roofs filtered out most of the engine noise. We figured it would be an alright starter place to raise our son until he was ready for grade school," I said.

"Place was on top of an estuary, meaning mosquitoes as big as this. The fuckers would hang out on the steaks you were grilling and suck the blood right out of the beef. The other thing about that apartment was how hot it got. Like stifling, like even with the windows open, except we never opened the winders because Patricia was afraid the mosquitoes would kill us in our sleep. Worst of all, the people before us never moved out," I said all spooky-like. "Beings, Del. Beings."

Del just drove.

"Well like I said, a presence. My kid saw it. One morning I'm holding him over my shoulder, trying to get him to calm down 'cause he would never stop doing his sprints around the goddamn house and he says, 'Dad, Dad who's that? Who's that putting things away on the shelf?' So I spin around ready to throw fists cause this place isn't in the greatest neighborhood, being near the airport and all, but not only is there no junkie gang trying to take our TV, but there's no shelves either. I made sure to check because you know it could've been a shadow, right? The next second, I swear to God I hear a voice say. You're not buying this, but I hear a voice say:

'Balp.'

I'll tell you right now, I almost dropped my kid. I almost jumped out of my skin."

"Balp?"

"Yeah. Very matter of fact. A woman's voice and I heard it in my mouth. Not in my ear. It was like someone was talking into my mouth.

"I struggled to tell Pat about it, but she didn't believe me. The fighting got worse. She wasn't nice anymore, like how she was with the restaurant customers. Whatever, you know. Pat finally tells me how unhappy she's been and says, 'You're an idiot with a chipped tooth from fucking stupid Woodstock '99 and you have permanently bleach-wrecked hair. No one's going to love you and that includes me.'

"Thank Christ my sister lived about three hours away up in DC. I moved in with her until I got back on my feet. Still getting back on my feet, if you ask me, right? So I'm packing up my shit and I take my blinds because I paid for those blinds. With every pound of sun shining in I see on the wall super faint slot marks where shelves would fit. So I'm thinking, does our kid see people's spirits or furniture spirits or both?

"I told Pat, but she didn't care. She was always pissed at one thing if it wasn't the other. Not my fault. That apartment fed off relationships, if you ask me. Turned people into its gloves so it could do what it wanted with them. Because the crazy part? The crazy part was the people who moved in after us got themselves involved in a double murder. Guy stabbed his roommate straight in the thigh with a screwdriver over their Xboxes. The roommate played dead until he bled out and was actually dead and then the other guy stabbed himself with the same screwdriver to make it look like a fight. Bazinga. Total murder central, man."

"Rough," Del said, pulling off the highway.

"Craziest thing is the guy died like four months later from some rare pathogen in his roommate's blood. So really we're dealing with someone killing his killer. Anyway, I dodged a bullet with that place. Glad I got out of there. It was just a bad situation."

"Do you see your kid?"

"Still lives with his mom down there. Second fastest on his track team, last I heard. Probably even faster now," I said.

The steering wheel wavered in Del's hairy ass palms without him bringing the van anywhere intentional. All I could really see from the side were the yellow lenses of his goggles. No reaction at all. *Heartless inmate prick. Fine then.*

"That's nothing," he said.

"Nothing? I don't think that's nothing. I think that's pretty heavy shit. I think you are underreacting to everything I just told you." I checked our phone to see that Shaun Rice II left a voicemail message responding to the smiling photo I sent of us. *I can tell you're way off-route because I can see you on my fuckin' satellite,* he said. *You need to get your faces out of that town. You're gonna get sniffed out.* I didn't listen to the whole thing. Shaun Rice I is to the point. Shaun Rice II talks himself in circles.

"I had a kid," Del said. "Well, it was a dog. But pretty much a kid."

"Yeah?"

Del stared straight ahead as if watching his whole life go by in the windshield. The air went tart with signs closing in for 'Seaside' this and 'By the Sea' that. I could feel my lungs were turning to shreds.

"Yeah. I'll tell you the story. I'll tell you the story of how this happened," Del said, pointing to the thing stapled above his ear.

"How you shave your head?"

"No, the cochlear implant."

"I hadn't noticed that," I lied.

"I used to drive for a latex supplier way back when. Mallory worked second shift at Saint Judith's. She took her smoke breaks every day around one in front of that sign, SAINT JUDITH MEMORIAL in big letters, like the sign was about her. I'd be off-loading and she'd shoot me those looks; you know, that half-asleep look girls give you where their face gets all Garfield-like. So we get to talking, this and that, until eventually, we're going on lunch breaks at the same time. We're sharing chicken nuggets in the Burger King parking lot. You know, people-watching and mixing dips. Next thing I know we're pretty much living together. We're buying barbecue sauce, we're mixing it with mayonnaise, bing bang boom. She moved fast, let me tell you. We adopted a terrier and named her Bin after my grandfather. Bin even kinda looked like our kid. Had my muzzle and Mallory's knotty orange and white hair."

"Sorry, are you saying Ben?" I ask.

He says, "Bin. Like a bin." There's a sourness in the air, a rot coming in from the cracked window. We pass a seafood shack with plywood nailed over the walk-up window and a mermaid painted on its broadest side.

"Life was good. We even had a cover for our spare tire that said it. Most weekends we'd grab a twelve-pack and find somewhere to drink and identify wild cabbage. Mallory loved identifying plants. Especially wild cabbage.

"One day, we all go for a drive. Bin loved going for rides in Mal's car. She'd sit right between us. Car usually broke down, but it didn't this time. In fact, it was running extra well because I just replaced all the belts. Thing chewed through belts. So we drove real far to a trail in Vermont or Dakota or one of those states. We figured, it's a nice day, we'll do a hike. Never trust nice days. Mount Summer, Mallory called it. 'We gotta climb Mount Summer,' and I was like 'yeah we have to do that' even though it's this completely flat, soaked ass swampland.

"She wanted to hike back around the bog because she swore it's where there was a waterfall she saw as a kid and waterfalls tend to harvest cabbage behind them. I told her it was too far out for my shitty lungs to handle. There wasn't even any cabbage, let alone a waterfall or a slope for a waterfall to exist upon. By this point, we're pretty far out. Not that we were too worried about getting back because it was still our honeymoon phase, on top of it being one of the longest days of the year, so shit was on our side. Hey, what's wrong with a little adventure, we thought. Adventures, you know, being lost together, it can be pretty romantic. It was so romantic in fact, that I carved Mallory's name into some tree bark to show her how serious I was. But then hours go by and we're wandering around and Mallory's getting worried. I'm carrying Bin because she's too tired to walk on her own. Mallory's freaking out, saying maybe she didn't come here as a kid after all. Maybe it was a dream she had. We can barely walk so we look down at our shoes and we're wearing sandals. We remember raw chicken is marinating in the car. There's an entire gallon of punch. There's potato salad. We were on our way to a barbecue for her pregnant high school friend, not a hike. Something compelled us to go there."

"Car must've reeked," I said.

"It was not a right swamp. Nothing right about it. A pre-WWII swamp. Mallory and I got messed up in something messed up," Del said. "And we never got back to the car. We didn't. Not ever."

"What are you saying?"

The two of us became trapped as cypress trees, right in that swamp. Let me tell you, it was the silence," he said pointing to his left ear. "All those years of silence did this."

I laughed, but then Del said, "No, I swear to God. Bin stayed by us for a while, bless that dog. She waited. Howling like I didn't even know she could. Three nights she waited by us until this old fisher bear comes up and she runs away and I'm thinking she's done. But she came back and lived off the swamp. Eating moss. Eating shit. Shitting water. Fighting those fishers. Eventually though, eventually she was gone."

"Trees. You turned into trees."

"I saw seasons turn over again and again. The wind bent our backs. Screamed in our faces. There'd be people too, because civilization grew up around us, you know how it does. We felt kids carve junk into our bark and watched those kids grow up and confess their secrets because they thought they were alone. But let me tell you. None of us are ever alone. Especially not in the woods."

"What'd it feel like?"

"You know when the dentist shoots you up with Novocaine and it seems like you could bite through your own cheek?"

"Yeah."

"A little like that."

"How'd you get out?"

"Fell one day. Probably after, I don't know, fifty years. Maybe seventy-five. A hundred."

"So where's your girlfriend? Did she fall over too?" I asked.

"Mallory? Nope, she could still be there. Maybe not, who knows."

"You didn't try to find her?"

"No, no, of course not. How could I? Place doesn't even seem to exist. I checked all over this internet. It's not there. Goddamnit to shit."

"What?"

"We missed the gulch," Del said. I felt the van's brakes tense up. Up ahead was a sign that read PUBLIC BEACH PARKING. He slowed the van, pulled diagonally into a space, and cranked the shifter to the right. We left the van in the deserted lot, save for a few cars. May to September it was twenty dollars to park. Now it was just sandbags and shells that people ran over. There was a second seafood shack, also with a mermaid painted on the side. The scales of her tail fin were chipping off to become turquoise mulch. Just past the boardwalk were gray heads in windbreakers, walking with their hands in their pockets. We went toward the ocean which was a blank line glittering above the bleach of the sand.

"These places," Del said. "Bay towns, I mean. They'll suck the blood right out of your dick. They live off dick blood."

"Well, okay, I don't know anything about any dick blood." I checked my own phone, making sure there was still a charge, as Del was crazier than I thought with these enchanted bogs and I thought maybe I'd have to call the cops out here.

"Let's wash this shit off," I said.

We tried the rinse showers in the beach's restroom, but nothing came out when I turned the lever. As Del tried fitting his head under the sink faucet, I went to throw our burner phone away in the toilet. Above the stall was a sign indicating that it was a composting toilet and under no circumstances should garbage be left in it. I stood over the black opening. A network of spiderwebs just above my hair soaked up the shit smell. I stared deeper. There was only darkness inside. There were eleven new voicemails on the burner phone. Del was saying something. I dropped the phone into the hole, listening for the sound of it hitting ground, but the sound never came.

Outside, sandbags were stacked next to the lifeguard chairs like fat-filled pillows. The ocean growled at us when we neared it. It sent freezing bursts of wind that rattled signs warning about the shark and algae-infested undertow. Signs for ticks. Signs telling us not to disturb some nesting bird. Underneath

24

the bird was a circle that contained a crossed-out dog. In defiance, several people were walking their dogs and kicking sand over the meat cigars. With nothing but weather in my mouth, I watched an old-timer swinging his metal detector over the beach, wind shaking his oversized windbreaker. Across the bay, I could make out a smoke signal drooling upward from the mainland.

Del stopped me.

"I gotta tell you something important," he said. "It was the other way around in that bog. It was Mallory who fell first. She never came back to check on me after she was free." He approached the old-timer.

"Anything today?"

"Today was no good," the old-timer said. "Last week was good. Found a ring. Wedding band seems it. Could be a class ring too, except those are less valuable."

"What else?" Del asked.

"Coins. Shaving razors. The usual."

"Doesn't sound half-bad," I said. "You got your own little treasure."

"Just need enough to buy a stronger detector. Then I'll really be able to sniff out the goods. Best thing I ever found with this thing was Vera Wetherspoon's hiking boots. Wearing 'em right now."

When I looked down to check, I saw he was in fact wearing extremely small boots.

Del narrowed in. "Those really Vera Wetherspoon's?"

"Oh yes, sir, she detected the rivets," the old-timer said, motioning toward the wand. "It's written here on the tongue." He crouched down to reveal a crudely drawn name. "They were buried maybe three feet down like someone tried to hide them. See? Vera."

Del carefully inspected what was written on the tongue. "That says Lara something or other."

The old-timer seemed, at last, to act like we were disturbing him. He looked to be making up his mind and then reached into his pocket and revealed what I thought might be sea glass but wasn't.

Del's eyes widened. "Is that what I think it is?"

The old-timer grinned. His nose hooked over his whiskers like a drunk Muppet when he did this. I wondered if he noticed our jumpsuits and was pretending not to. In the next moment, Del snatched the metal detector from the old-timer and before confusion could register on his face, the aluminum stem was broken over his back, batteries and plastic flying in every direction.

I reeled to see if anyone noticed. "The fuck? There's people around," I said.

Del scooped up what the old-timer dropped, which was green but not really.

"No, there's not." He approached the sea and hurled the souvenir in. It punctured a coming wave, turned to froth, and then was gone. The clean snap of the bar against the old-timer's back felt like puke in me. He wasn't getting up. His leg, also made of windbreaker, twitched. The yellow drool freezing on his whiskers gleamed a little in the sun.

Del followed the object's path, stomping as he entered the water and trying to keep his knees above hissing surf even though he was nude. I thought about taking off my uniform to fold it beside his, which he had left crumpled.

"Get in the water," he said. "Don't be scared."

It would be safer to enter wearing my clothes. Most of the asbestos was embedded in the fabric now anyway. But Del was right; there was no one else around to see. Even those stragglers by the jetty, they weren't who we thought they were. Del braced against an undertow, aggressively rubbing froth over his head, soaking the battle between eel and manatee. Wave after wave crashed on him, flattening long white spindles to his body. I thought I might as well join him in there.

HULLS

When Bethany used to bring her husband for get-togethers at Rita's house, Rita's bichon, Lieutenant, would eat raw carrots right out of their hands. After finishing dinner and getting a little drunk, they would go for walks in the woods out to a bog. Rita's husband would usually get a fire going when they got back, which made her voice raspy. But the hearth was also a place where shoes could be left to dry if one of them had accidentally been sucked into the mud a little. When Rita's husband passed, a few years before the bichon, a propane-powered fireplace with decorative logs replaced the wood stove. It kept the house warm, almost as her husband had. Lieutenant was cremated. Not in the fireplace, but his ashes were kept on the mantle above it.

Every Tuesday morning Bethany and Rita took their walk. The route was traditionally a two-mile pass around their neighborhood that ended where it began. This was a time for gossip and the revisiting of things they told each other the previous week. In June, Bethany left to stay with a dying parent in Ormond Beach, so there had been no walks. Rita tried walking alone, but she couldn't help from talking out loud, and it began to make others in the neighborhood uneasy, so she made juice instead. She bought an extractor at the mall, along with bags of spinach and apples from the supermarket. With Bethany gone, Rita saw a two-month gap where noticeable changes to her appearance could be made. An opportunity to show her productive use of a passage of time. Rita started adding ginger to her juice and would display the roots on her kitchen windowsill. Her home became adorned by purposely placed novels with matte covers. She bought a Roomba from Amazon.

Bethany was considerably impressed when she returned from Florida. Both with how clean the floor was and with the gadget's charm.

"What's its name?" Bethany asked, standing inside Rita's living room. The plastic horseshoe crab chased a path towards her bathroom, whirring louder on the tile.

Rita laughed nervously. "Well, I hadn't thought of it. I forget he's there most of the time."

"He is cute, isn't he?"

"Florida must've been unbearable. The heat," Rita said, changing the subject. It was easy to dye such places in a poor light.

"It was what it was." Bethany shrugged. Once again, Rita felt bridged to her friend and the thought left her renewed.

A car accident was reported that morning, so their walk was now with purpose, their stride a little more pronounced as an audience of rerouted cars floated by them. Bethany and Rita concentrated more on their dispositions. The portraits they made. According to the radio, the crash was severe, with one vehicle colliding head on into a utility pole. Some neighbors on the opposite side of 87 lost power. Rita and Bethany knew exactly where it happened. It was a bad spot, where the estuaries of cul-de-sacs drained out to the main road. Sometimes you just had to take a blind leap of faith. A woman died there three years ago, which people still liked to talk about.

"You do look slimmer," Bethany said. Bethany was really the one who had lost weight. Her eyes sank into her head and her old fall jackets wrinkled at their seams. Now she couldn't walk without stopping to push her bracelets back up her wrist. Rita wasn't used to seeing her friends pick up new habits.

"It's just a Braeburn and a handful of greens. Maybe I'll drop in a little ginger or mix in some chia seeds."

"Really, you've pared down to nothing. It seems like so much changes after being gone."

"You didn't miss anything, it was quiet," Rita said.

They hadn't talked on the phone while she was away, so Rita broached the subject of ill parents very carefully. Through rumor, she knew Bethany's dad was improving.

"It was just the flu this time. But—he isn't going to get any better. I'm not being pessimistic. This is the reality of it." Rita felt a tinge of dread at the thought of her friend moving away to stay with her dad, as this is what people often did when parents got old. She would have ample time to make juices, but who would be there to see? The mall walkers with their atrocious sneakers? Both of Rita's parents died when she was in her thirties. Her husband followed a couple decades later. Then Lieutenant.

"Can you believe that?" Bethany motioned towards a lawn, cropped to the skin as if it were preparing for battle.

"They've always been showy. I know Jan thinks we all care so much, but who is really looking at her lawn, really?" In the driveway, a man hurried into a sedan with his tie trailing behind, chasing something invisible. Caught in another dimension.

"There's Jan's husband," Rita said.

"He looks about the same," Bethany said.

They felt flaunted before the parade of cars. The attention was something new and relished. People rerouted from their normal paths, checking their phones for directions or calling in late. Neither woman was accustomed to so many guests at once.

"How is Seth? I feel like I haven't seen him in so long," Bethany asked

"Well, he's fine. He's working today," Rita said, carefully examining her street's borders.

"Still at Lowes?"

"He's got about a month left. He even met a girl there. But then he's going back to landscaping part-time with his uncle." The sedan joined the detoured traffic and Jan's husband waved a stiff palm at them. Rita imagined Seth courting a girl in a little blue vest, twirling her gum by the raw lumber, but then thought that kids don't really chew gum anymore.

"The dentist's daughter?"

"No, no this is a different one. He might do another semester down at the community college," Rita said.

"QVCE?"

"River East – where Filene's was."

"You know I keep hearing good things about their programs. Nan's kid went there, she's going to study nursing," Bethany said.

Rita already knew this but pretended it was some new revelation. From the bank of roadside litter, she picked up a spent, miniature bottle of liquor and pocketed it as if it were an arrowhead.

"Whaddaya got?" Bethany asked.

Rita displayed the artifact in her palm and carefully studied her friend's reaction. Bethany was a woman who now spoke from the contented, orange places that they both used to mock from their porches. Rita thought Bethany could exist as one of those state-of-the-art dishwashers or a plastic fern from Hobby Lobby modeled after something a wealthy missionary brought his mistress back from taming the Congo. Bethany wouldn't be able to leave again if she were made of polyester designed to look like bromeliad foliage.

"We're getting close, do you smell that?" Rita said.

"The rubber?"

"Yeah."

"It smells awful." They wrinkled their noses.

"That's a handsome zip-up," Rita said.

"Thank you," Bethany said.

The arrows of brilliantly emblazoned DETOUR signs showed visitors how to leave forever. Rita huddled into herself for warmth.

"I could see you there." Rita stepped back as if imagining Bethany cast against a different background.

"Where? Florida?"

"Yes, you could land a nice, charming widower. Live out your days in those see-through yoga pants."

Bethany laughed heartily, "Oh, I can see it." Both sighed at the same time without realizing the other had sighed. Blue lights peered through the spindles of branch and foliage. A wrinkle of smoke in the air peppered with radio chatter.

"Oh my goodness."

They watched the tow truck churning up the hill. A boar, massive and starved, ambling toward its kill. Police officers kept their hands on their hips. From behind a stop sign, Bethany reached in her pocket for a cigarette but realized she had quit smoking. Draped over the car was a clean white linen.

"Look at that. How awful." At the top of the utility poles, the power-line transformers surveyed the scene with their permanently unimpressed faces. Rita was wary of them. One of the poles was splintered at its trunk where the car made its impact. The others were tilted as if mourning their wounded sister.

"And look at that, there are no tire marks. Means he probably hit that thing going full speed," Bethany said. The veiled car reminded her of a crudely sewn ghost costume.

"Just awful." First responders were sweeping plastic and glass into the long mat of road humus that had accrued over time. With Bethany standing there rendered helpless by random, unavoidable violence, Rita made up her mind. If her friend was going to settle down, it wasn't going to be as a juicer or a plant. Not the old toaster oven that only cooked if it was whacked or the hallway runner that still clutched mud and animal dander, but the dehumidifier in the spare bedroom.

The froth of the day set and turned yellow. Rita went home, where her little robot was making its way onto the carpet. She bent to give it a pat that it almost seemed to pause for.

"Who's a good boy, Lou." It continued toward an end table to inhale the remains of a rice cracker. She crumbled an extra measure for him.

"You're rambunctious today."

As the hearth, Rita's husband pouted. "You be quiet," Rita said. No response came from his ceramic logs, crossed indignantly. The stove was a place where wolf spiders found refuge from the woodpile as it deteriorated into a dune of rot. The spiders that lived in the wood had migrated to Rita's cellar to breed, with any exiles now filling the belly of the Roomba.

"I'd miss her too. I really would. But I doubt she'll leave us anytime soon." The Roomba bumped into a wall and readjusted its scanner. It chirped happily, rediscovering old paths.

"A juice does sound good right now," Rita said, separating the hull from a sunflower seed.

The last volunteer firemen returned to wherever they came from. A stream of traffic opened to commuters driving up the hill without any idea that anything had ever happened there at all.

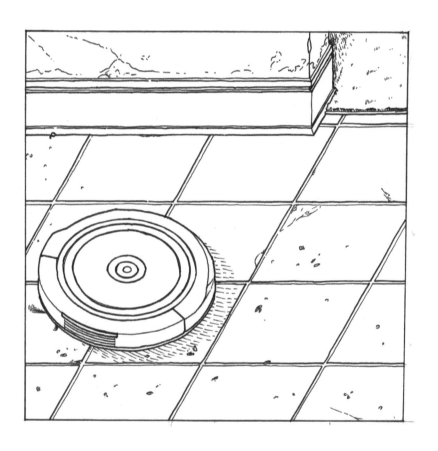

IRENE & THE LEVIATHANS

"So there's this sea hag girl just minding her own business.
All day she sweats around her cottage, using exotic vinegars to dry out shells
and root vegetables and hydrangeas. She lives by the shore. Cape Cod or
someplace like that. She was banished to live there by her colony because,
well, she's a witch and that's what they did to witches back then. A kid went
missing so the colonists are marching to her cottage with hatchets and chains
and that sort of stuff. I swear one of them was that guy from *Home Alone 2*,
but I haven't looked it up yet. They walk through the permanent fog right
up to her front door where she's already waiting for them, you know, with
a hood over her face. All of them look at her with these disgusted looks
and they crush her vegetables and drag her off to the beach. And then the
minister, who I think is the Home Alone guy, starts reciting something he's
written on his arm about casting devils back to the fathoms and devils taking
over the bodies of frail women. They're all gathered on the jetty where they
chain her in a coffin doused in whale fat. Oh, but before that, they pull the
hood back and her face is all messed up and she's got this tiny eye and rows of
see-through teeth. She's all, I'm going to return in four hundred years for the
lives of your descendants or something like that. Then they torch the casket
and float it out to sea. Wait, hold on."

Irene moves the phone from her ear to her shoulder. She's curled up on
a couch, washed in lamplight when the door unlocks. A figure reeking of
rushed smoke breaks and seafood walks in and drapes a sweatshirt over a
corduroy recliner, sheathing the ghost of somebody else's grandfather asleep
in the chair forever.

"Don't eat anything on the stove yet," Irene says to him. "It's not done. It
just looks done, but it's raw, so don't eat it. So, yeah, they burn her body and
four hundred years later we see the beach again, except it's all summer homes
and surf shacks and kids trying to stop their ice cream from melting too fast.

You see this woman with her goggles and shower cap, breast-stroking way out beyond the buoys, you know, like, getting her exercise, when a shark just fully tears her leg away. She's floating there all crooked and the shark keeps coming back for more — it's so gross, but yeah, it's the witch. She comes back as a shark to terrorize the shore for the summer. Then somehow they figure out a way to stone her to death with like a million tons of waterproof marijuana. No, you don't have to put Mom on. You sound tired so I'll let you go. Okay. Alright. Love you. Yup. Bye."

Irene's phone is replaced by a remote, in surrender to an uneven sleeper sofa. Netflix loads on the TV and for a moment the walls run red.

"Were you telling him about *Sand Witch*?" A voice with a joint or cigarette between its now human teeth says from the kitchen. Irene asks for a charger. The owner of the voice returns with a cereal of leftover coconut shrimp and stolen pasta sauce, a glass of pink Minute Maid mixed with scotch and a paper towel that he folds neatly on his lap. He shuffles around in his baggy pajama pants. His name tag says 'Ahoy There! I'm Forrest.' A swordfish stitched into his breast pocket watches over the rusted swamp on his plate. Irene's not asking about his day. "Wait. What is this? Is this that *Blackfish* documentary? With SeaWorld and the mamma whales?"

"I don't know. It autoplayed after," she says with renewed interest in her phone.

"Nope, nope, no way. Everyone always says this is way too heavy. And I mean, I'm around tortured fish all day, right? So why would I want to see more when I get home? Why don't we just watch another *Sand Witch*? The fourth one's supposed to be good."

Irene has stopped paying attention. She's texting her girlfriend to convince her that the dinner she cooked will be good this time. "I gotta shower in case Larissa wants to do butt stuff," she says, pausing the stream and floating away with a crumpled blanket in her wake.

Forrest considers giving their house ferns a little of the pasta sauce. Each plant bows as if struggling to survive under an impossible weight. He tells them they don't have it so bad. Tuesday night means Irene is shaving her legs, which means he'll have to be alone with Larissa and pretend to be interested in her art history thesis. Forrest shovels the last coconut shrimp into his mouth, but as he hears designer hiking boots hopping up the stairs he realizes that it's too late.

Her hair is pale magenta and she's got cat lady glasses and she has four or five Miller Lites in her. "You smell like you're still working at Red Lobster," Larissa says. "You still working at Red Lobster?"

Forrest makes a deflating sound. "Yup. I'm a manager now though. So."

"I'm not surprised they take you so seriously, what with that beard you got going there," Larissa says. She stretches out across the couch and lazily claps her toes.

"And Billy Fins bought it, so I mean, it's not really even a Red Lobster. It's much nicer, actually," Forrest says.

Irene brings a fog of vanilla into the living room. She makes a note in her mind to cancel her dye appointment when she sees Larissa's new hair.

"Here, I brought these beers. The soapy kind," Larissa says, cocking a six-pack slightly askew.

"Man, thank you so, so much," Irene says, embracing her and crumpling a floral skirt. "I love this, where is this from? It's Savers isn't it you son of a gun."

Forrest refuses to surrender his chair, insulted a soapy beer wasn't offered to him.

"Good goddamn is this *Blackfish*," Larissa asks, cracking open a bottle with her keychain and flicking the cap on the rug. "This movie. This movie is so important. I watch this all the time."

Their downstairs neighbors fight in muffled Serbian trespassed by English. Forrest strains to listen but he's diverted toward killer orcas. Neon wetsuits and dorsal fins that dip below turquoise waters envelop the water in his eyes. He's too tired to fight it. The screen finishes them off one by one. Several empty bottles cover grinning catalog models with rings. Irene asks Forrest to grab his stash because —

"You've got better drugs and you still owe me for your share of the gas bill."

They pass a bowl around resembling an iguana's head. Nothing kicks in until well after the epilogue text.

"I've never even been to SeaWorld." Forrest is locked to his chair by some unseen force.

"You know what? Like fuck that," Larissa says while folding her arms and leaning into Irene, now drawing nothing but fumes from the lighter's fluid chamber.

"It's alright," Irene coaxes her, inventing a constellation from Larissa's arm freckles with her fingertip. Trying to pull her back to the material world. "This guy is beat," she says while laying the iguana to rest on the table.

"But someone should do something. Like, they can't get away with that," Larissa says. "There's probably a petition online."

"I'm finding it." Irene unfolds a scuffed-up MacBook.

"No, no, no," Forrest says, his sweatshirt half over him like a blanket. "We gotta, like. Something bigger." He mouths *bomb* and makes a chucking motion with his entire arm.

"You've been on Reddit too much," Irene says. She struggles to rise, but Larissa gets up first and stands before them with the laptop. A motivational speaker clad in pawnshop floral.

"Yeah, we should. Here, wait." Larissa holds the computer as a drunk au pair would hold an infant. Her fingernails clack over the keyboard.

"The fuck is a pipe bomb?" Irene is exhausted. It is starting to get late and she has to clear space in her mind before speaking. "What are those bottles with towels in them? You know, you light the towel and throw it."

"Oh, Molotov cocktails. You want to Molotov cocktail SeaWorld?" Irene watches Larissa's cat glasses drop malevolent shadows on her brow.

"Well, no, that's where the animals are," Forrest says. "We don't want to hurt Tilikum. We have to access the problem's source."

"What if we feed Jim Atchinson to Tilikum?" Irene whispers. "Tie him up and slather him in canola oil so he goes down nice and smooth. Yeah, we'll kidnap the guy. I'll lure him to a hotel bar with my lady charm and slip something in his drink." Forrest begins to ask what Jim Atchison is.

"The Caucasian male CEO with the three-hundred dollar haircut, profiting from the park's nefarious business practices," Larissa says.

Nefarious? Forrest knows her type and considers telling her she needs to pay rent if she's going to sleep here so much. Those trust fund punks with their Seven Sisters-bought vocabulary. There was a time when he used to hang out all day at cafes taking things in and out of his Amazon cart too. The ones where the baristas roll up their sleeves to showcase tattoos of geometric lines and succulents. Forrest thinks of the graying doughnut shop next to what was a Red Lobster. The moray eel inked into the afternoon shift supervisor's headskin. But then a different thought occurs to him and his body races from the room.

"This is simply another business. Just its own medium of greed." Larissa's eyes go wide, sending the shadow away. "Like, someone should do something."

Forrest returns with a glass skull.

"Isn't that Dan Asteroid's vodka?" Irene asks.

"Yup." Forrest displays it proudly. "Imagine filling this bad boy up with gasoline and chucking it right through that Atkins guy's living room window. This is exactly the type of moment I was saving this for. I stole it from a party in Bangor last year."

"You don't go to parties," Irene says.

"It was just like, a get-together," Forrest says.

"Here we go. Jim Atchinson. 184 Sycamore Cove Drive, Orlando, Florida."

"Fucking typical."

"No, but we have to. Like tomorrow. I don't really have to go to class, I don't think." Larissa looks up as if the answer was written in the water stains on the ceiling.

"You can skip grad school classes?"

Instead of letting Larissa answer, Irene asks Forrest if they can borrow his car. He weighs this and sets his skull on the floor. Strange, stoned logic of a seafood chain shift leader.

Forrest makes a prayer formation with his hands over his nose. *Dead-See-Eee-Oh.*

"Orlando's only twenty hours from here," Irene says. She had visited family friends there as a teenager. Recalling the humid insides of roller blades charms her and she feels euphoric in the memory's spell. Of summer heat instead of heat from a radiator. Imagines herself far within an orange place that curdles as sugar across her cheeks in an unexplained form of phantom tanning. "We never do anything we say we're gonna do," Irene says through a yawn.

Bass plods from below, where the Serbians are now practicing the calls of swamp mammoths. Irene and Larissa clear a space on the coffee table and start drawing on a paper towel, a map from Maine to Florida. They check the weather. They look up cheap lawyers just in case. They draw a white male with sharpie devil horns and a goatee.

"I think the couple downstairs is full-on fucking right now," Larissa says.

"Do you remember that guy from Whole Foods with the backward mustache?" Irene asks. But Forrest is already asleep.

"No one really notices all these drownings because they happen over such a long span of time," Larissa whispers with closed eyes, speaking from a dream.

"That's it," Irene says. "I have friends down there." Irene swallows whatever soap remains, and it courses but does not swim to somewhere deep inside of her.

She wakes to the sound of vomiting. To what could be someone pouring minestrone into a shallow puddle from the bathroom down the hall. Irene rolls over to empty bedsheets netted in pink hair. Larissa and her boots have snuck out.

In the driveway, the sun feasts on black sweatshirts. Irene listens to a voicemail, pacing between their overflowing recycling bins. The parents at the bus stop across the street scoff at the Dubra bottles. She turns her back to Forrest, but he can still detect the strained apology in Larissa's voice. "This is so stupid," Irene says. "I knew she'd do this."

"Do you still want to go?" Forrest asks. They lean against his champagne pearl Honda, considering whether their plan makes sense in the daylight. He pulls something wrapped in velvet from a Kohl's bag. Kids at the bus stop hit each other with their backpacks and laugh in triumph.

Irene looks down at the vodka bottle shaped like a skull.

"That's our son," Forrest says.

"She's such a flake, you know? I hate that." Irene concentrates on scraped whale flesh and neckties. She turns the glass over in her hands, feeling the firm, yet delicate cheekbones. The liquid eye sockets. A school bus turns the corner. Its shifting gears still pang dread in their stomachs.

Forrest says, "So at this juncture it's probably too late for either of us to show up at our respective places of responsibility, right?" The yellowness of the bus is churning another bout of vomit in him.

"You know what?" Irene says.

"What?"

"Let's go to Orlando," Irene says while shooting her finger through the air to point down the street.

Turn off all appliances. Forget to water one plant. Drown another straight from the tap. Before locking the front door, Irene decides to abandon the beard clippings in the bathroom sink, empty bottles on her nightstand, and balled-up paper towels. If they never return, these things will be enshrined in the museum built in their honor.

Irene leaves donut grease on the display of Forrest's stereo. She wipes the rest on her jeans. The freeway's drone and the occasional swerving over the rumble strip is a comfort they'd both forgotten.

"Standin' on your Mamma's porch, you told me summer lasts forever! These are absolute, perfect receptionist anthems," Irene says.

Forrest cracks his window to release some of the music. "What are receptionist anthems?"

"It's like, I don't know. The receptionists wait for vacation in those offices with their radio and muddle over targeted banner ads for resorts. Constantly taunting them with sloppy, drunk Jacuzzi sex."

The highway throws them further into the South as their bomb watches from the backseat and wavers with the swells of pavement. More childlike than threatening. When Forrest closes his window, their apartment's burnt candle dust returns, and so he leaves it open.

"Those Jacuzzi bubbles will travel right up your vagina and kill you. Right to the bloodstream," Irene says.

"I don't care. I need real food," Forrest says. They assess their options from a complimentary Citgo periodical that also advertises cheap diesel oil and snowmobile insurance. Irene grazes pages that feel as though they've always been damp.

"Look at this. Eight bucks gets you a large popcorn, medium drink, and admission to a full-length movie. Maybe these nachos in the picture too," Irene says. "A gritty reimagining of *Three Men and a Baby* is playing in half an hour."

"Way too spooky, my friend. The house where they filmed the original *Three Men and a Baby* was cursed as all fuck. A kid there died from polio and he didn't even have polio."

"Is that true?"

"I don't know, man, probably. But exactly one hour, thirteen minutes, and ten seconds into that flick you can see, clear as day, the fucking apparition of a child. I don't want to be there when the kid finds out he's not in the remake," Forrest says.

"Reimagining."

"Whatever."

"Okay, well, *Tueur* is in fifteen minutes," Irene says. "The Montreal Tribune says it's *March of the Penguins* meets *Anaconda* meets *A Christmas Story*. Oh, but it's in French."

"No problemo. I took a year of French in middle school." Forrest says.

The theatre is off Exit 81, somewhere near where two different color states start oozing into each other. They park in a plaza also inhabited by a tired-looking Cantonese buffet, complete with a birds nest inside one of the neon sign's burned-out letters. *Tueur* is spelled out on the marquee but is missing the first U. Neither mentions SeaWorld. It hangs over their heads with the phantom vowel. The kid selling tickets says to enjoy the movie, and they tell him the same. Irene says they found a bargain, even if greasy men in the audience are talking to themselves in greasy voices during the whole thing and are checking over their shoulders to see if Irene is giving Forrest a blowjob. For two hours, the darkness of the theatre and the popcorn butter on their fingerprints expels any past or future life.

After the movie, a blurrier world greets them in the parking lot. Forrest mentions it's a gut-wrenching feeling. The surround sound leaves a throbbing pain in Irene's wisdom teeth. The Honda's engine won't turn. Its windows won't go down and they start to drown in the smell of the synthetic butter clinging to their sweatshirts. Neither of them really remembers how they managed to get this far out of state. Irene says that Florida will always be there, and besides, how do you even fill a skull with gas, let alone decide which of them would throw it?

Irene pleads with a local garage over the phone, her tongue nursing the back of her mouth. Prodding at a cockroach wing-thin kernel. She leans against the beached vehicle before drifting to a farther sidewalk to make another call to someone else. It's just closer and easier to turn around than it is to keep going.

The end of Forrest's beer is orange blood. He tells Larissa about things secretly thawed in oil used for deep-frying shrimp. They've returned to the eye of a two-bedroom apartment on a street framed by frost. The skull looks on from atop a speaker tower, poinsettias stuck through its brain hole. It has a couple new scratches. In the kitchen, Irene struggles with a Christmas skillet cookie recipe while Larissa multitasks between her phone and a semi-annual holiday lingerie catalog. She tells Forrest the perfect ass has just a hint of cellulite. Something about Photoshop and art school in Rhode Island.

"I think my boss is gonna tap me for the new franchise in Augusta. He's been putting me on like every weekend schedule," Forrest says, haloed by a wreath doused in cinnamon stick Glade. From the kitchen, it sounds like Irene is talking to herself.

"Who is she always on the phone with?" Larissa gives up on the bras for a moment.

"It's her dad," Forrest says.

"Her dad? She never talks about her dad. Let alone to him. I thought he was dead."

Forrest lowers his voice to a whisper, jubilant to be able to confide in someone. "Her dad was trying to lose weight before the holidays a few years ago. He was going to surprise Irene and her sisters. This was when Irene was still in school. So he's out on his morning jog and he just slips backward on some sand, you know, like how they put on the roads when it's icy, and lands right on the back of his neck. That was it. Just totally fucked him. Poor guy was comatose for a few days. The whole deal. Now he has permanent brain damage and doesn't really follow everything. Even though he has no idea what's going on, Irene would still tell him about her life. Until, you know, she kind of ran out of things to say."

At first Larissa looks as if she has swallowed something angular, but whatever it is stays well hidden. "Man, I wouldn't mind being him," she says. Forrest exhales at a fern that is now beyond saving and the camera pans out slowly.

"All this boy wants is to spend his summer at Christian science camp. Instead he gets stuck at his family's vacation cottage in Connecticut. The cottage is on a lake, and in the lake there's a monster," Irene says through a torrent of steam. "But it's cool because the whole thing was a nature documentary. You know how *Planet Earth* has that godly voice drawing parallels between a beetle rolling a dung ball and a lion about to take down a gazelle? It was a lot like that.

"We open to a kid's first day working on a Pequot dairy farm. The steers are dying off. Some kind of infection or parasite or something. He has to help get rid of the dead cattle in a bog. The farmhands insist this bog is totally haunted with haunted beavers, haunted algae, haunted wild strawberries, or I think they're strawberries. Do strawberries have thorns? Whatever they are, they're growing there so people won't go near the swamp which is friggin' deep, like abyss deep. That's why the farm uses it as a dump. Everything just disappears. The farmhands bring rifles with them but it's like the 1940s so the kid doesn't give a shit or ask why they need to be armed for a cow funeral. Oh, and this isn't the main character, it's a different kid. This kid's about to be the first one killed. Of course, as they're dumping the cows in, something weird's stirring up the water. Then a cow gets snagged on a branch and they tell the kid to knock it down. He's like, 'I don't think so,' but they're like, 'it's fine,' and of course, he slips into the swamp trying to knock this cow leg off the branch, and then everyone's shooting at the water until all you can see is smoke and flies.

"After that, a river is diverted to flood the farm and the whole entire town it's in. The townspeople are depressed because they don't want to leave their homes. Some of the stubborn old folks even off themselves. But the basin is stocked with plump bass and these nice new cottages are thrown up, so the town gets forgotten about pretty quick. The only reminder is in the middle of the lake where there's an island that was once a hill the town kids sledded down in the winter."

Dishes are shifted in a stainless steel basin, where the drain is clogged. A grease rainbow wobbles on the surface. Irene abandons shipwrecked skillets with reefs of batter clinging to them.

"So the boy, the one stuck at the lake cottage, befriends a gang of local teenagers. They're basically just these girls who follow around a James Dean lookin' ass guy, who the boy idolizes. You know, with the beater and greased-backed hair. One night they go skinny dipping. Jimmy Dean swims out too far and gets pulled underwater in this big, gross Jacuzzi of blood. He seemed immortal so it's especially horrible for the boy. And the narrator's voice is calmly describing what's happening as if this guy's death is just naturally part of the lake's ecosystem.

"Everyone's devastated. To cope, the teenage widows fog themselves in marijuana. The boy stops eating. He loses all his baby fat and stops giving a shit about Christian science camp. He falls in love with one of Jimmy Dean's widows, a polka-dot bikini girl named Eloise or Matilda or something. Her mother is super overprotective. Like she won't leave them alone. It's the Fourth of July neighborhood picnic and everyone's watching the sky, waiting for the fireworks to start and the mother's watching the boy, making sure he's not about to try anything funny but he's definitely about to try to kiss this girl and right as he turns his head the girl's mother gets snapped under the lake. Fireworks flash across their faces as they look on helplessly. The narrator is whispering about guts drifting out into water lily roots. About young love. About lifelong taste aversions to egg salad.

"When summer ends, the boy moves away with his family. Like twenty years go by where he goes off to college and finds a career in the city. But no matter what, he never lets that summer go. It stays with him even as he tries to forget it. Meanwhile, the narrator is explaining how a shifting ecosystem affects the lake community. These cute 60s cottages deteriorate into bungalows haunted by rednecks with sparklers and beer koozies, polluting the water with their jet ski gasoline. The wild strawberries are totally plowed over to make room for new waterfront properties. It's actually kind of neat to see how the architecture evolves. A few of the houses look like Grandma's, with that A-frame, cabin-chic style. Then an arm washes up on the beach covered in scum, but you don't really know who it belongs to. Do you know what a lentil ecosystem is?"

Irene turns off the burner and sits alone in the kitchen. Passing cars can see her silhouette in the window. Baby shower and wedding invitations from last year plaster the refrigerator. She stopped putting new ones up a long time ago. Synthesizers drift up from a Serbian radio station and she is a gargantuan, solitary thing floating in yellow.

"The boy reluctantly inherits his parents' cottage along with a lifetime pass to lake rights. Plus now he's got his own kids and wife in tow. Of course, the guy's totally paranoid, though, so he builds an in-ground pool to keep his kids the fuck out of the lake. Everything seems fine. There's even a drought. As the waters recede you can see the church steeple from the former town with herons swooping in and snatching up bass from its roof, until it rains for, like, days. The lake is engorged way beyond normal and then bam, you see it. A snapping turtle the size of a Joe Deer rider mower. Rips a drunk hick right out of his snow tube.

"See, no one really notices all these drownings and disappearances because they happen over such a long span of time. They just say the lake has been cursed forever by Puritans. Oh, and there's another part where the boy runs into his old polka-dot bikini girlfriend working at a Dairy Barn and she's totally strung out on pills because they both saw a turtle murder her mom when they were young. You can tell that her life has been rough. She is a manager, though.

"Finally, summer turns to autumn turns to winter and the lake is frozen solid. The community goes dormant. It feels safe, like nothing else bad will happen. The boy is an old man now, his wife long dead. He's religious again. Every night he sits in his chair, watching a rifle mounted on the wall like it's his TV or something. When they zoom in quickly, *ghost mess* is etched into the wood. It has nothing to do with the story.

"The narrator is going on about trophic levels, Christianity and prey decisively confronting its predator, while the old man is walking across the ice toward that island. He pauses at a cavern marked by beer cans and used fireworks. He's tired now, so he's struggling down into this lair, using his rifle as a crutch, trying not to slip on the ice. And there it is. The serial killer turtle. You never really see him until the very end. *A plated armor varnished by algal blooms, riddled with musket pellets and scrapes from broken oars. Husks of freshwater-born vegetation sprouting from a landscape of parched and cracking mud, like a slumbering black planet deep in hibernation.* This animal took so much from the old man, yet he sets the rifle down like it's a gift and walks off.

"Now it's starting to snow a little, and as the giant floating faces of every person the turtle killed fade into the pink winter sky, an orchestral Christmas score rises into the bass line of "Maneater." You know that Haulin' Oats song? All while the old man's shuffling over strawberry vines stuck in ice, back through his own footprints. You know, it's just closer and easier to turn around than it is to keep going."

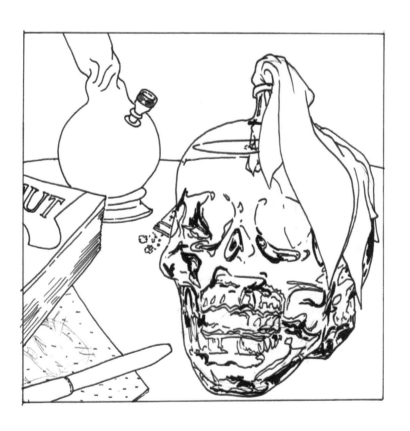

WORSER

Give it a dollar, put a dollar in its bowl, Winona says and she limps away to find better things to take pictures of. Others from our tour are putting themselves into the cherubs of walruses that have had their faces removed to house ours. Liberty is drifting as if on rotten blocks. Her crown stops right near my shoulder level. Picture the glitter on its cape burning in February's awful bleach. That silver thing who had posed with his fist beneath its chin has gone missing. A queen and the cowboy from Toy Story now sway on its cobblestones. They're trying to start over and repopulate. But there are rules, Todd, about doing it in Airbee & b's. You're a guest, you are not some wild western pioneer. Many of us were conceived in hotels.

Hurry up and take the picture. A Tennessean from the tour rips open a granola bar, cracked AC/DC logo stretching across his bosoms. He told me reptile facts earlier on the bus. Liberty is waiting for something. I can see my terror swirl in the oily lenses of her sunglasses. The kind your 5th-grade bus driver wore when she looked at you in the mirror and told you to siddown! The first pocket comes up empty, save for a foil shell that was once ripe with flavored gum. Zesty Cobalt. Maybe Spiced Arctic Winter Chill.

In the second pocket is the lint touch from old money that has been heated by a GE and folded in the birthday cards of a hundred teenagers. Feels like a five. What if it's a twenty? I'm pretty sure that's all I brought. Lord, thank you, Liberty has turned to pose in a picture with two cut off jorts speaking to each other in Alaskan. I'm struggling to remember the difference between how a five feels and how a twenty feels. A rattlesnake can live for three years without its body.

Winona is tilting her phone against the sun so it splays out in flares. She warned me if I showed the characters anything larger than a ten, they'd think it was for drugs. I pull out a fiver, yes. Liberty is back at my side and we are both looking out at the landmark. Here you go. As I let her steal the bill away I can smell her eyes; shallots, Sprite and the gelatin of Advil. Creases search up from her chin. Not paint. I'd like to join Winona but they're closing in. Queen Elsa from Disney's Frozen prompts a male tourist to take out his phone and she grazes a fresh manicure on his shoulder like a spider trying to drag a chicken bone. They hurry off behind the porta potties.

Picture, picture the statue of liberty says, voice the hinge of that one cabinet you're always terrified to open. Woody's collar is wet. I can see the veins in peach bronzer. There are no zippers or seams for a mask. Who are you, what do you need? Conton? Shoke? She repeats it back to me. Picture this place when it was new. Can you? The tour is leaving and I think they would abandon me here. Elsa is moaning curses upon a warm and comforting shit-breeze. She's taking what she wants to be the surrogate from some bald man from Pennsylvania. His family throws feed at the seals. I cannot provide them enough money. Howdy, stay with us there are snakes in my boot.

SOUVENIR

Getting to the Manor in Lisa's dad's old Taurus was a chore in its own right. Wet denim is a whole 'nother beast. It's twill bison with sand setting in its claws. A braying ox with cataracts so strong you can't see anything past the twin grey of her eyes. Lisa and Toby both warned about wading in with clothes on but I could barely hear them over the triumph ringing in my ears.

Taking an artifact from the mansion put something new, something savage in me. I marinate in hope. Sodium stings every single undiscovered cut and abrasion. In my other pocket is the four hundred dollars I saved bussing tables at J. William's Dock House where they reuse the stuffed quahog shells. I am rich beyond my wildest imagination.

The story of Dreyfus Manor is etched into the bases of commemorative sculptures overseeing the pay-for-parking lots. It's small talk for tourists between their drink and entree orders. Dreyfus was the only beach mansion in Wautuck that wasn't razed by an early autumn storm surge in the 1930s. Early autumn and late summer can be the same thing sometimes. Hurricane Nancy was tropical Halloween weather that came from nowhere. Just as the money from textile mills turned into rows of waterfront Victorians, the hurricane found the coast like an Ouija board's roving oculus. Impossible hotels with pillars and turrets and the timber for half-finished seaside mansions disappeared. Nancy took everything back with her to the horizon, along with thirty or so unlucky people. The rip current, an underwater river, took the rest.

Now the Manor's Grecian carved floors are sand and dragged-in mattress, with bonfire craters that breed aluminum cans. When it was a hotel for bums, one fire burned out of control. It scorched out the basement, giving the first floor its permanent stench of thyme on roast beef. There are shadows that have been there so long they've stained the corners.

The mansion is the eminent battleground for Killer Soldier. A rite of passage where sophomores hunt each other with Super Soakers. The name drawn from an ancient football helmet is the name of your target. Sometimes the Super Soaker chambers are filled with urine, and sometimes pink lemonade to resemble the urine of someone who's been kidney punched. If the target is drenched within seventy-two hours, you advance to the next round. But they must be really drenched, not just misted. It's got to be a fatal shot. Winner gets three hundred dollars. Technically, the game was banned by the parents because with all these kids roaming around, junkie car burglars figured out they could have free range over our neighborhoods at night without anyone noticing.

My brother knew a kid who spray painted a mural of a huge boobed priestess brandishing a sword in Dreyfus Manor's upstairs master bedroom. He's famous. As soon as everyone finds out what I took he will be a footnote in this town. A certain musk sticks to our clothing. It's a new kind. The unpaved road jostles us around so our words jut out like decaying mix CDs. There's only one working seatbelt in the back so I tell Toby I'll be the sacrifice. Lisa rolls her window down and says she's going to puke blood.

"This Yaz is trying to kill me," she says.

"It hardly affects me. Plus my mom says if I stay on it, we can eventually get a bunch of money. Some class action lawsuit or something," says a girl in the front seat whom I don't really know, but I would guess is called Hoarse Neck. Her voice rasps like a lung cancer victim speaking through a much younger vessel. I feel if I have to stay in this car any longer that I'll puke too and I don't want anyone to see what I ate. There's enough secondhand smoke engraved in the upholstery that we'll all probably be dead in twenty years anyway. My window is up, forcing the honeysuckle outside to seep in through the vents. It's too late in the season for fireflies. This recollection won't have any magic to it—I'll maybe put them there in a few years when I look back. Insert flashes, like people who take photographs in cemeteries that develop with floating orbs. Our bodies are somehow dread resistant tonight, even with the New England jungle wearing dusk as its mask. Even with the plastic glow in the dark vampire fangs Toby is wearing. We turn a corner and the rivet in my jeans digs right into my leg. Right into the tendons.

"Our whole fucked up country's in trouble. Something's about to boil over, man," Lisa warns us all. Our eyes graze in the rearview mirror. Clumped-on mascara and hair fogged red with dye infused shampoo. One fist on the wheel showing off a rock collection of bracelets. She's the only kid I know who drives at the speed limit.

"This solo right here, listen to this solo," Hoarse Neck says. We pull up to a swimming hole. Someone has spray painted '667' and 'desaparecido$' on a trout population control sign posted by the DEP. The fresh air renews me. Toby whispers that Hoarse Neck's shirt is see-through and she's being derivative, but I don't think he knows what derivative means. No one cares about drum solos or almost nipples, anyway.

We roost on boulders painted by more graffiti. I recognize some kids from school, tipping cans of beer and chucking empties into the dark. Their hair has grown out to rest over sunburned shoulders. I can tell everyone is whispering about how quiet Lisa has gotten ever since her dad got caught going down on their housekeeper, a Hungarian pastry chef with skin tags under her eyes. According to the rumors, she sued their whole family for sexual harassment. Now Lisa's dad sells printers at Staples with kids my brother graduated with.

The sophomores sit with hands in their kangaroo pockets without speaking to one another. The ones drying off after being killed are the only ones who are free.

"Anybody want a s'more?" Another senior who I've never seen in my life asks around. "You should get that checked. Looks like melanoma," he says to Lisa. Someone points out I frown exactly like my older brother.

"Brann Hueller looks like he has an ankle growing from his neck," Lisa says, pointing to a scrawny boy who last year was paunchy and always smelled like smoked meats, now planted in between two dreary-eyed girls in wet hemp bracelets. Brann is talking about how in three years, tidal patterns will bring the drifting bodies, dead from Hurricane Nancy, back around again.

"She's absolutely breathtaking," Toby says, watching Hoarse Neck devour each s'more ingredient raw. Brann and his girls slink away to conceal whatever they're about to do in the forest. Lots of people have left and we question just how long we can occupy this night. Toby tells me Brann used to jerk off to oil paintings in our Art History textbooks. Bodies don't wash up. Pieces of the houses as driftwood. Things the bodies owned, maybe, tumbled, to be returned all polished and smooth.

I dig deep in my pocket to take out my keepsake. "Hey Toby," I say, and his drunk mug takes a few seconds to comprehend what rests in my palm. Flashes his lime fangs. I stash it in the same pocket as the money. Toby watches the space where my hand was. I tell him not to tell Hoarse Neck or Lisa. He asks where I found it. I can see him exploring Dreyfus Manor in his head. Scanning all those corners splotched with body juice, washed out when rainwater comes through the roof. I know one day the mansion won't exist, so I should appreciate its grossness now. I tell Lisa when I'm older I hope the people who build a timeshare on top of it invite me over for cocktails. If not, I'll have to drop in and say I used to live there.

"This town is nothing but a church. It's a big church that worships the beach," Lisa says.

I know Lisa is stoned because she's repeating what the drifters scrawled on the floors of Dreyfus Manor, in an Ace Ventura voice. I hadn't noticed she was passing a spliff or that anyone was even smoking. It's possible she's pretending to be stoned to fit in, like how I would when I was younger. Lisa says the town had survivor's guilt after the hurricane, which is why they kept building and covering things up. The strange senior chokes on the spliff. When he sucks in again, I can see he looks to be about forty years old. He says Lisa is right. That the town is burying its past.

We point the Taurus towards town and end up at 7-Eleven. A Crown Vic's parked outside to ward off any would-be robbers. An automotive scarecrow. Hoarse Neck gets a hotdog, then throws away the hotdog and plunges the bun into a make-it-yourself strawberry milkshake. She tells me about the little mites every company uses to dye things red now. She says they taste delicious, in her moth-eaten native tongue. No one is listening. For a second, I can smell thyme mixed with propane wafting inland.

Just as we're about to leave, a guy in a red polo walks out of the bordering liquor store. My arms burn when I recognize underneath the baggy, dye-stained skin around his temples and stubble that it's Lisa's dad. More sunken than I remember. None of us say anything. He strolls right by and either doesn't notice us or just chooses not to. Us in his former car. In his former backseat. I picture his morning commute to Staples, veiny hand dangling out the window where Lisa dangles hers. Questioning where he's going. None of us admit what we've seen until Hoarse Neck eventually turns up the music and whisper-sings to it. She tells Lisa where her cousins are going to school. People I've never met.

Something keeps me up while Toby falls asleep on my shoulder. Safe in his seatbelt, like the big, wide-eyed infant he is. Is it the musk of the mansion still hanging on me or the voices of Nancy's victims? Sweat, briny and cooling, drenches the pictures in my head until I no longer recognize them. Lisa says she longs for a time when homeless men roamed Wautuck. She asks where they all went but I'm pretending to be asleep so I don't have to answer. When we turn on the heat it pushes out something dead from last winter that makes me sick to my stomach. It doesn't pass until I close my eyes for real.

It's midday when I wake to the hum of a vacant house. My jeans are draped on a radiator that hasn't been used in four years. I stand on the front patio in my brother's bathrobe. The air is too heavy to hold in. Storm clouds, bulging with violet, simmer just beyond the mall. For now, the afternoon is bright, the day stretching before me like the back of some great jungle cat in a blacklight poster. On the mantle is my trophy. My souvenir.

A tropical storm warning screeches from my phone. Other phones join. The neighborhood's breath is staggered as it tries to speak above it. But there's laughter too, from kids chasing one another in the street with citrus-colored guns. The boy builds the pressure on his Super Soaker until the pump won't budge. His shot misses and he signals a time-out to rebuild. A girl spins around with her own pistol drawn. The boy stops laughing. Pause, he says, we're on time-out, but she's moving closer and she's squinting now.

THE TREE

My Uncle Bruce lived in a trailer park near an ocean where all the motels had a mermaid painted on their front sign. He was a ropy version of my dad, but with the same overbite and denim jacket. He didn't have money, but he was smart. Everyone knew he was smart. They always said it was a classic case of unapplied potential. A classic case of one brother flying right and the other going south to Florida, until migrating back up the coast to follow a candlemaker named Sylvia Brown. Everyone said he told you things that were true. My mom said it was what made people not want to stay around him as much.

It was May when my family went to the shore. A stagnant pond-water kind of May that makes the legs of your pants feel terrible. We rented a duplex on a street called Osprey Lane and my parents talked about how Bruce must've thought it was off-putting that we didn't stay with him. Our cottage wallpaper was made to look wooden. The old woman next door fed her cat uncooked hot dogs.

"The whole reason we came out here was to be close to Bruce," my dad said in the car.

His brother suffered from an ulcer. I saw drawings of them at school— little flesh volcanos attached to walls of stomach lining. I saw them in the barnacles on the totems dividing up the saltwater.

"It's because he used to eat limes like they were apples," my mom said.

His campground was off a gravel road lined with orange metal dinosaurs, breaking up the earth for new buildings. There were maybe three porta-potties with locks hanging off them. I'd always wanted to use a porta-potty.

My parents were dropping me off on their way to a casino. They said it would make Bruce happy to hang out with his nephew and gave me a sandwich along with twenty dollars for ice cream. My mom waited in the car while my dad shook his brother's hand and they surveyed what was around them with their hands on their hips, squinting at faraway things.

"You were this small last time I saw you," Bruce said, boring through morning humidity. I remembered him with earth in his knuckles and a blanket over his car seat. Less round of a stomach, but I didn't tell him this. I imagined the barnacle inside his body, a canker sore feeding off citrus.

He seemed to know everybody at his trailer park. Women with freckled sunburns asleep in folding chairs. Men who wore wigs. "Meet my nephew. He's going to be eleven." Some just waved while others took my hand to shake it. He showed me the whole park, pointing out how the gypsy caterpillars were eating the Japanese honeysuckle. "An invasive eating another invasive."

I asked him if he'd ever seen a tornado and he said that was just on TV. We visited a man named Hewitt, who had a broken lawnmower. He paid my uncle forty dollars to repair it, and we left him sitting with his feet in an inflatable pool. I helped bring the lawnmower to my uncle's camper where we sat in the grass. Bruce spat at different filters for a while as if they were birthday candles.

"You have a girlfriend?" He asked.

"Nope."

"Better off for it. I had a girl here. She had that kind of hairdo like the lumbar of a wave," Bruce said. "Biker tattoos. Left with a fuckin' shoobie. Some rich guy."

"I've heard that before," I said, though I hadn't heard that before. I took out my sandwich which I thought would make me less thirsty.

"There's an ass for every seat I guess," he said. The lawnmower growled to life when he yanked its cord. "Why do you have a sandwich? Your mom give you that?" He took the bleached white square tightly encased in Saran and crumpled it into a molten baseball. The lawnmower petered out. "It's summer. You cook outside in the summer. Come on, we're going to the grocery store." By grocery store, he meant a cabinet where he kept lemon-scented Pledge with several guns.

It was the first time I went hunting. Bruce carried a rifle and he tasked me with carrying a bucket and an empty revolver I stuffed into my belt. Crashing through the underbrush, my thirst turned to hunger, and then it felt normal to be out in the heat, finding things to kill. I asked him what we were hunting for, but he didn't hear. My uncle kicked at bushes and squinted his eyes up at branches. He was getting frustrated.

"We gotta nix a squirrel and by George, there are no more squirrels here," he said. "All the construction is probably scaring them away."

When we got to a Private Beach sign I felt hopeful, thinking we were about to see naked people, though no one on the beach was really naked. In the shells displayed over the sand, I saw the fancy plates my parents would throw at the ground whenever they got in a real argument. They looked like someone was paid to polish them. The people there, sunbathing or reading novels, cut scowls at us. I thought this was maybe due to our heavy clothing or because we had guns.

"'Nother shortcut," Bruce said. "Ignore these people. They're all dying anyway."

We trudged right past a hair-backed man patting pebbles into an alligator he had formed from sand. He mumbled a horrible swear under his breath as we passed, right in front of both his kids, who laughed. Sand became dirt became pine needles became leaves captured in green slush. After a long time mucking around the woods, we stopped at a lagoon where the air was soaked in fish grease. Here there was an entire field of boats with the names of women rotting off them. Some of the propellers were still caked in seaweed. Some were being pulled to the earth by green demon arm vines, which was a type of vine I invented. Meaty horseflies came down on us in the open light, stealing my blood in such small amounts that they thought I wouldn't notice.

"It's a boat cemetery, kid. Bet you never saw a boat cemetery before. Ocean used to reach all the way out here before it cowered away. Only mud now, probably forever." My uncle gripped the steel marble on his rifle and slid it back. "Squirrels love it here."

Before I could voice my objection, a blast discharged from the barrel, followed by an immediate ringing in my ears along with crows and the patter of raining wood chips and horseflies crashing into themselves in retreat. He fired again.

"Got him."

My uncle skinned the squirrel and affixed twine to its carcass before lowering it into the brown water. "This is how we catch crabs," he said.

"Are there squids in there?"

"Oh yeah, there's squids. Little ones, but they're in there."

After disappearing the squirrel, we waited, not talking but listening to how the stillness moved. A canvas-topped boat sprouting berries groaned at us. When the string was taut, Bruce pulled it out to reveal a cluster of blue crabs, jittering robotically and clinging to the squirrel flesh which turned white and lured more flies. I thought about how the squirrel woke up that morning not expecting this to happen.

We took a different way back to avoid the crabs spoiling, passing through fatter trees that stood far apart as if they didn't talk to one another anymore. In the bucket, the crabs were ready for a fight. They glistened like firecracker popsicles, clicking and frothing from their hard mustaches.

"Don't let any sun get on 'em and keep the water sloshing around in there," my uncle said. "As soon as a crab takes the count, poison floods his meat. A dead crab will get its revenge on you pretty quickly too."

I made sure to protect them as we walked, avoiding divots like how my dad drove whenever my mom was carsick. Among the trees, there was an especially hairy one with bark that boiled out in brain-like scabs, a mess of vines spilling off its tentacles. It was a sixteen-armed god caught throwing spells in every direction. Watching us pass or maybe allowing us to. I realized we were walking faster.

It was a relief to be back in civilization. I got a better look at the porta-potties. There was a newly parked cement truck. Its back was a lot like a shell and I almost said this to Bruce because I thought it was clever.

"Rabbit food and jazzercise, according to my good friend Pat Gable. Health clubs make bank near an ocean. Smart if you think about it," Bruce said.

Back in the yard, I fulfilled the duty of rinsing each crab down with a garden hose. The mud they once hid under dried out just as it hit the grass. My uncle allowed horseflies to feed on him as he hummed to our catch and scrubbed them clean with a black bristled toothbrush. He then used the hose to wet a paper shopping bag, filled it with the crabs, and told me to leave it in the freezer. "Best to put these fellas to sleep first. You ever tasted an animal's last thoughts? Those nightmares are nobody's business but their own."

Over the largest stove burner, we roasted our catch in their skeletons and ate them outside on my uncle's patio furniture. The woven backs felt good to weigh against after our hunt. There was buttered vinegar coating my fingers that I decided I'd never wash off. My uncle brought out four beers, disregarding his ulcer. Two beers were for me. There was no grilling. I decided I'd keep my twenty dollars. I had a shoebox half-full of saved bills back home.

When we finished eating, Bruce shut his eyes. I shut mine too while we listened to a chamber of frog throats. The beers tasted like Christmas candy from my grandmother's basement. It was comforting to know just hours before we had been inside the perfectly blacked-out wilderness behind us. Even the beach and its miserable people, the prehistoric animals, porta-potties, and the lagoon were all absorbed in the night now. I fell half asleep to the thoughts of these places. I made up a dream about the boats in the graveyard being alive until Bruce woke me from it.

"The tree we saw earlier."

I knew exactly which tree he was talking about. "Yeah?"

"You're not going to like what I'm gonna say."

"What?"

Even though I could barely see him, I could tell my uncle's eyes were still closed. His speech seemed measured around the night critters screeching from the woods.

"That tree is going to be what kills you. I can't tell how or when, but it's going to have something to do with that tree."

I laughed. He kept quiet for a whole ten minutes until finally, I found the courage to ask how. Bruce said he knew things, and he knew the tree we saw would ultimately be responsible for my death. Nothing more. Being a child, I was not used to adults speaking to me so matter-of-factly and figured he was playing at my imagination.

"I hate to be the bearer of bad news, but you knew it too. How we stopped at it? I could tell. You knew. It was looking at us too. You have what I have. Up here." He pointed to his greasy, see-through hair.

"You're fucking around," I said.

He sat up in his chair and said, "I would never fuck around about something like this." We were both cursing now.

"I'll just, I don't know. I can avoid it," I said. "Or we can go shoot it. Tomorrow."

"Have fun shooting a tree, you weirdo," he said.

"You have a chainsaw, don't you?"

"Hey, I wish it was that simple. But I'm afraid it's not."

I asked him what he suggest I do. My uncle thought about this for a second.

"I'm just the messenger," he said. Peepers chirped slower with the morning's raw creeping up on us. I noticed Bruce had accidentally kicked over one of his open cans and let it lay there.

I thought of the boughs being cut down, its evil spreading about the world as weapons in wait. A toothpick after finishing a blind date, the thing lodging itself in my throat. There were the branches hovering over the road every morning on my way to work. A single plank rotting in a windowsill. A paper cut, becoming sudsy and infected by yellow lichen before I lectured to my classroom. A crooked stair in a house that I almost always trip over. I thought of chopping the tree's family into firewood, knowing full well it would try to burn my house down. But I would already be outside. Safe through every thrown splinter.

Bruce lurched over, positioned the can upright, and flattened it with his bare foot. "There's not a lot you can do. Not with these kinds of things."

My uncle was killed by a series of strokes, first taking his voice and then control of his face before finally dumping wax into his heart. The ulcer had only kept him company. A friend that died with him.

It was hard to remember where exactly my uncle's trailer park was, but I did eventually find it sleeping behind a place where they rented jet skis. The motels were bigger now and entombed in siding made to look like salt and pepper shingles. You could smell the acid when the sun shone on them.

The private beach was now public. It seemed so much smaller, which might've been from the parking lot they'd built. A sign warned of shark attacks: WHERE THERE ARE SEALS, THERE ARE SHARKS! The faces of the seals in the photographs resembled human skulls. From the forgotten trailer park, I went through the woods to the grove which was now overtaken by grass and deer ticks. There I found a stump to sit, but I couldn't make out which one was or had been the tree.

After a while I got back up. It was here I tried to see things that were far away and placed both hands on my hips, if anything just to have something to do.

FRANKENSTEIN, NOT UMA THURMAN

You were Mia Wallace for Halloween and I was sexy Harper Lee. 'How to fake blow' stained the search history under the spider web cracked screen that cut up my fingers where I typed my name into your phone. I wasn't even planning to leave the house, but stoned in bed with headphones digging into the pillow is not where friends are made. Dancing at the church party, we saw four other Mia Wallaces, each with blood running from their nostrils to the bleached spores of their mustaches. I thought we'd reek like fog machine juice forever but it left our clothes the second we stepped outside into hurricane season South Carolina. Into pie crust cooked with yams already purple at the edges.

"Don't worry, I'm easy to forget about. You won't even notice I'm gone, I promise," was what you said, but it was all glitter sleeting from the band of my bowl cut. It was all wet palms.

The next year you were Frankenstein Mia Wallace. Same wig, white buttoned-down, and blood, but with cucumber skin that made you look seasick, finished by a surgical scar you drew from one corner of your forehead to the other in your Taurus's visor mirror. An expert on pretending with baking soda. On glued-in bolts. Here it was agreed upon that we were the kinds of people who bail and eventually there would come a time when we probably wouldn't talk anymore. Realistically, most people who are friends now won't still know each other in five or so years, right? It's just how things work. Two Halloweens is a good run, let's just appreciate that. But then the makeup became real. We found out you were allergic to cheap face paint that night and for some reason, I obliged when you asked me to take an Instagram of you in the hospital bed. True devotion to the character. Method acting in a wing of Scorpio babies born under another tropical storm.

By the third or fourth Monster Smash, I asked you not to watch over me if your dream ever came true. That recurring one about a poisonous grasshopper biting you in the field behind your parents' house. It was narcissistic to think you'd want to follow me around when you had the galaxy to explore. We still shook on it. I wouldn't try to find you and under no circumstances would you ever, in a million years, come back to haunt me.

There were no more costume parties. There were gaps. There was returning with a sketchy tattoo of some non-existent planet, which was a logo the city branded on you. You drew re-imagined Disney princesses in Photoshop while I stayed at home, making fun of you to my friends in our fathers' armchairs. "Miriam used to be normal. She was cool. Remember that?" Before you were seized by tall buildings and drooled back out an entirely different person. Jeggings to high waisted jeans. Dust to dust.

I heard it happened driving home from your parents' house in the Pennsylvanian woods. You swerved to avoid hitting a deer and your Taurus ended up upside down in the empty river, blood rushing to your head to rush out of it. They tested you for chemicals, but only found shrimp scampi in your stomach because that's what you always asked your mom to make. Your dad began to feel something again from the Classics of Rock Pandora station. He will spend the rest of his days hunting for deer. Avenging your death with bottle upon bottle of buck urine.

It had been over a few years since we talked and the person you were to me was made from different parts. Frankenstein, not Uma Thurman. Only the traits I chose to recall, branded cattle-iron style on the rosy sirloin of my brain. You said, "It's all about authenticity. I know the incision mark is there, even though it's covered by the wig's bangs." I thought a lot about the Scorpio kids born when we met and how they were all old enough to run away from home now or hide up in trees. I thought about how during the early morning hours of November 1st, a hospital is the weirdest possible place you can be.

I didn't go to your stupid wake. I heard they played an acoustic cover of Van Halen's "Dance the Night Away" like it was a g.d. trailer for an erotic thriller. My eulogy would've involved the shrimps trapped in your belly that you decided to take with you. They were going down with the ship, into the barren tributary of the Susquehanna. Miriam would do that. No one would've gotten it except us.

But these were not things we said. These were not things that happened at all because I don't go to Halloween parties and I don't think you'd be the type to either. Rather, I stayed at home in the dark to watch *Baywatch* on my laptop, and during a quiet part, I think I heard your sneeze. We didn't make it weird, though I knew it was you. The actual you. The kind of person who, no matter how much they spit in your hand, will ruin a pact.

SPOILING THE CERAMIC EATER

I first meet Carl Dean while leveling a cigar in my after-dark sweats, "My Blue Ridge Mountain Boy" listless on the turntable. Its call comes out of the brush pile then, just around dusk. GLAK GLAK GLAK, it whispers sharply as if from a creature being confronted.

"What kind of creature are you?" I ask. "Is that what you are? A creature?" Everything outside Village at the Willows responds with a fertile silence.

For over seventeen years, I've been the duplex property manager here. Even on the windiest of days, you'd be hard pressed to find an ounce of chop in our swimming pool. We don't lock our doors. Safety has draped over Village at the Willows like a sweater, covering each corner while the rest of the world lays outside in its own filth. Lydia Reynolds, three porches down, refers to us as living in 'brick' units and I must always correct her by reminding her that we live in 'brownstones.'

Far enough into the outlying brush, enough that you can't see from the lawn, is the compost heap. It's where Christmas trees lay scandalously with broken bird feeders and where Folgers turn to new dirt with the banana peels and eggshells. It's a burial ground for parakeets and other pets less than eight pounds. The resulting mud is mineral rich with low acidity. Everyone is allotted four buckets of soil for their gardens, and I just know Marin Alvisio from 36B is taking twice that. You should see her hydrangeas. Most tenants use it as their personal landfill, throwing away their garbage at night when no one is looking. But I see them.

Until one day, I don't. There isn't a cracked watering can or basket to be found. Every broken flowerpot has disappeared. Only the faces of jack-o-lanterns glare back at me underneath chickadees, gossiping as if they saw everything that happened.

As much as I'd like to investigate further, there are more pressing things to worry about than missing trash. I must have a stern talk with Mr. DeSanto, five porches down, because I found his son's greasy face prints on my door and last week I heard shuffling around outside while I was folding laundry in my bra. Now, I'm well aware that teenagers need their jerkoff material, but a menace cannot go unpunished or there is no telling how far the fabric of the community will tear. Fabric is all we have. No one is home when I knock on the door, or maybe they've just drawn the shades and hid. In any event, I take their welcome mat and I throw it into the forest.

None of my neighbors bring up the missing trash, though I am pleasantly surprised to see a tenant has taken the initiative to clean up our community a little. Ever since women started rushing off to work at the close of the seventies, the family dinner table has failed, and when the dinner table fails, the home follows in its wake with the whole neighborhood not far behind. My suspicions lie with Lydia's daughter who visits every other week and cleans up around Lydia's unit, making sure she's taking her meds and not letting the mail accumulate. This despite the fact she's also stealing newspapers from me.

But I'm wrong. A few days later I'm raking up grass clippings because the goddamn landscapers are on drugs, and I hear GLAK GLAK GLAK again from the edge of the brush. Within seconds I'm indoors, and that's the last time I ever see the rake. The next morning, it's gone with the welcome mat.

I've become that old maid who feeds animals and I chuckle at the prospect. It fills me with a warm, golden goo. I give him a name: Carl Thomas Dean, after Dolly's husband. "You are so hungry!" I tell him, unsure if he's listening. At night, I don't dare leave my lights on. If I can't see him, then what right does he have to look back at me? When I check the dumpsters, all trash seems accounted for. Carl Dean is too scared to venture this close. Such a careful thing. That is, unless he's simply a cavity in the ground. A pit that digests whatever is thrown in the mouth, casting its voice and sending feelers out for prey.

Marin Alvisio speculates that he was born from decades, or perhaps even centuries, of leaf mold and humus. She tells me this while we have toast and Liptons on her patio. Marin has severe dementia that comes and goes. I doubt even she knows what she's talking about. I say, "who knows how long they've been harvesting scraps here?" This parcel of land may go back to the early settlers, back when actual willows were roaming our little prairie. I wouldn't be surprised. Maybe Carl dean was always down there under the ground and was nurtured by all that rot until he decided to come out.

"It's the wolf trees themselves, who witnessed their sisters get chopped down and burned and acquired a taste for violence, who are now craving these things themselves," Marin says.

"You need to focus," I say. "Something very important is happening here."

For a week, things stay quiet until one morning when there's a message on the answering machine from a nice salesman. I hear screaming. True, bloodcurdling screaming. I burst across the yard to find it's just kids playing near the pool. My heart sinks.

Won't eat children, will you?

I'm hauling donations out of our Goodwill bin when Mr. DeSanto's son sneaks up from behind and frightens the living daylights out of me. I tell him the bags are mine and I don't have to explain myself to some creepy, dirt-lipped kid.

"It's going to bite your hand," he says. I drop the garbage bags, spilling their insides onto the grass. He says in his little voice, "Some soil remoras should never be fed."

I tell him to look. His dad is not going to be happy when I tell him what I know about his peeping through my door. I leave without the donations. Mr. DeSanto's son watches me until I am behind sliding glass, where I draw the curtain so tightly the seams collapse into each other like giant, wrinkled sheets of skin.

The next morning, I gather up my Tupperware and candles. Throw in a framed portrait of me from high school, a stew of ashtrays and extension cords, half-empty prescription bottles. I feed him everything until my home is nearly bare. I drag broken patio furniture from the storage shed and leave it all in a sacrificial mound. Something watches me do this. Not the chickadees. Not the sunflower taking root in a cantaloupe's skull. Not Lydia's daughter in her jogging clothes.

Just thinking about Carldn meddling around my sacrifice gives me gooseflesh, erecting the hairs on my arms until they pounce right out of their pores. Using my *Life & Style Weekly*, I bring myself toward climax, thinking of the elastic tongue getting thicker only when it laps at my legs. I close my eyes to see Lydia's daughter whispering something into her mother's ear. I make Carld drag their bodies to his compost pile and I don't finish until they've become a field of chrysanthemums.

Afterward, I have my cigar to chew on, just to taste the jolt of raisin and peppery leather; a meaty wrap clamped under my teeth like the grape leaves of Marin's imaginary youth she is convinced was in Rome, even though everyone knows she's from Milwaukie. Cardn paces my porch lights at the border. We anticipate each other, waiting for one to cross.

In the morning, I wake up with my head full of nightmares. Young DeSanto roams our lawn with an antique rifle from some forgotten war with which he wishes to prosecute my creature. I ask where his mother is. He points to the tree line but then shifts his finger toward the brush. When I wake up again, the sheets are damp. My heart is engorged with dread until daylight floods

Village at the Willows again. I unfold a lounger to sunbathe, but algae has turned the pool into a swamp. I have to spend my whole afternoon sweeping a net through the mire to clean out all the drowned moles and leaves, dumping bleach in until the container is empty.

When I go to cook my toast for lunch, I find the bread in the fridge is speckled with more algae. I'll need to have Marin drive me to the store. I try bleaching the bread but my bathroom cleaner is too diluted. To distract my hunger, I try a newspaper. It only reminds me how the rot outside Village at the Willows is trying to creep its way under our fences. There are stories about grave robbers hunting for LSD in the spines of dead people. Selling the bone acid to millennials for them to trip off their grandparent's marrow. A Rhode Island man spent hundreds of years as a tree. Hood dairy products are being sourced from the breasts of indigenous women in Burma. Kenny Rogers is a lizard emperor dying from scale cancer. But that can't be. I can hear him outside talking to someone. I crawl to the window.

"I was going to pick up a half pound of turkey," Kenny says. "Do we still have juice boxes?" Yes! It is unmistakably his voice. A real celebrity, here at Village at the Willows. I hurry outside to find a stocky man in a jumpsuit hopping from a van. With no regard to me, he starts putting around my compost pile with some kind of reverse vacuum on his back.

I yell sternly to him, "You are not Kenny Rogers."

"Got that right, lady," he says and deploys a pewter mist over the edge of the compost pile.

"Stop that. Who do you think you are showing up here?"

He says he was hired to exterminate the fruit fly hive, and I tell him I didn't hire anybody and I've been the property manager here for over seventeen years. This white trash land astronaut says this community has been corporately owned for well over a decade. He pulls a respirator down over his face so he doesn't have to talk to me. Mumbles something about there being no property manager. I tell him he's not making sense. My fists turn to shaking stones. I wait for Crdldn to appear and devour this uninvited guest. To kill him brutally.

The DeSantos move away without giving notice. Months go by. The portrait of me stays half exhumed in coffee grounds. The frame has been almost entirely gnawed away by my soil remora. My ceramic eater. Everything else is gone, with blacker earth accumulating over my face. Mrs. Alvisio has left a shrine of mums and dead hydrangeas which is very nice of her. She didn't have to do that. Any lingering chickadees have left, and the jack-o-lanterns, now deflated and bearded with mold, have full-blown ecosystems blossoming from their mouths.

Sometimes as I lay under my blankets, I'm sure I can hear GLAK GLAK GLAK, except it's no longer just outside. Cr_nl is devouring someone else's patio chair wicker. My hands permanently hold the perfume of corroded metals. His call dims more into the distance before disappearing completely. New Christmas trees melt with summer's cornhusks. Late at night, I can hear other things, so far off.

TRANSITION LENSES/CONSTANT FEAR

I'll blame it on Petra's mom. She never liked me and I overheard her once call my whole entire family Lake Terrace trash. Always complaining about the expired old folks she found when she cleaned apartments uptown. They're lurking all over this city, getting cheap rent on their kids' dime, but do they visit? No. Look, I'm not paid to keep them company or check on their well-being or make sure they're not mixing chardonnay with their sciatica pills. I'm sure as shit not paid to find their bloated corpses that's for sure, she'd say while Petra and I ate the KFC she brought home. Inhaling cartilage. The foamy mashed potatoes.

I guess it had been too long since something broke. There was a pang of dread swimming around in me and I'm pretty sure it was said that it was inside everyone who lived around here. They'll say she held a water grenade, sweating and squirming in her hand like a liver.

Sometimes the feeling will creep up so slow you won't even notice, Petra told me during winter break. Peppermint coating my tonsils. Gently at first, but with the momentum of a spirit gliding its toes across wood flooring. One of those outdoor barn ghosts that made its way inside. A fistful of stolen toilet paper. I'm telling you, it'll soak right up. What a totally depressing thing to say. Twisting and digging further when it becomes apparent this is the sort of heirloom that gets lost inside of you without ever finding someone else to show it to. It's contained in latex which is not heavy with water. Or at least not water from any tap you've heard of.

Once it happens everything's suddenly different, Petra said. Probably already planning her new friends. This is the day of reckoning when she's going to eat her words. There was a time when our schemes were something to be bonded over. We chewed the same piece of gum. Flicking it into some old witch's hair. Setting fire to cardboard in the dumpster in the alleyway between Princess Nails and the drug front deli. Watching its indigo smoke pour up into people's windows.

I can remember when porch light would stick to the snow slumped on our street. One long freeze that choked the life from front stoops. From open-air fruit stands. This was before Petra betrayed me. A simpler time, they say. The quiet has kept a ringing in my ear as synthesizer from an eighties monster movie. Living in constant fear of knife rubber dragged across my throat, to spew orange blood. This grenade could have melted snow from the freezer inside it. Kept there next to a slice of wedding cake cemented in plastic wrap. I think Petra went back inside through the fire escape. She's probably watching TV.

Her emergency exit is still propped open with a cinder block just as I expected it would be. I use the stairwell, making sure to move on the front pads of my feet, up towards her family's apartment. Unit 34C. I turn the handle real careful so as not to make anything clack. My heart is throwing the syrup of blood up in my ears too loud, following vacuum paths with the balloon held so tight I think it could burst. Their TV is on, I knew it. I knew there'd be tendrilled plants hanging everywhere and dishes soaking on the counter too. Petra's mother would always refer to her husband as her "beaux" and did nothing but sit around drinking SlimFast mixed with chicory coffee all day.

Ricki Lake is on their TV. Her guests came all the way from spit-country. From the boonies where they ride on dirt bikes to each other's houses. "We make bargains with the pasts we leave behind," she says from the audience into a fake microphone. A man called Stew listens while sitting completely still and clawing both of his armrests.

Being back inside their apartment seems like I'm moving on my own accord within someone else's fever. It's so different than how I remember. Reeks like cologne rotting on ground turkey. The sleepovers seem like they never happened here. They couldn't have. Strange teapots burned at their bases are scattered on the floor. I'm navigating over each one, arched and readying the shivering gelatin glob to smash it down on Petra's head. We make bargains, we make bargains.

When I peer around into the living room there's no one on the couch, but there's a figure slumped in the doorway. They are watching me with their sunglasses on. It is not Petra or her mother at all. Her apartment is 34B you idiot. Their couch was green. Their TV was bigger. It isn't water in the balloon. Stew springs from his chair and goes offstage.

JESUS VS. THE CREATURE FROM
THE BLACK LAGOON

This bonfire beach party situation was where they summoned him. Where a great, swift violence came and took us. All you need are coals, melted sea glass, a little harmonica and a sprinkle of ground beef, scorched to coral snot. Now we have a recipe for something that'll really get its germs in your shirt.

I came to Amityville with Ichabod Vance. Ichabod drew surfers. I was an ex-Ornithologist with a failed doctorate on the pack mentality of gulls habituating treeless spaces. As it turns out, I had a nonrefundable fear of open space. I found if I wore the right pair of sunglasses, the frames would block my peripheral and keep me safe. In Amityville, I was the only naturalist in a pond of artist types. It would be a fresh start where we were going to find ourselves, both Ichabod and I. How I got roped into a propeller accident cover up is beyond me.

The report goes like this: guy played a chords-only version of Elton John's "Can You Feel the Love Tonight" for a girl. She then sirened that guy into a low, moon sucking tide. This goes to show you can pick notes off in the dark all high and smiling, but the blackness can snuff you out like a blanket if it wants to. As the boardwalk tarot card readers will have you believe, the whole thing was very mythic. Between the smoke off the driftwood, harmonica spit, the moon and the salt, by accident or on purpose, it summoned something from another place.

In the morning, about three miles from an old World War II fort, Levi found the body. He was a cop so he was used to finding bodies. Her remains were badly sunburned. We crossed ourselves there on the beach before calling it in. Reception was shit that far out, so while Levi tried to catch a signal, I had to stand and wait with the dead girl.

"I'm real sorry," I told her.

"It's ok," she said. Black-tailed herring gulls hung up in the sky, probably with bits of her in their stomachs.

"Life you know, works out in weird ways."

She didn't say anything else.

The official report the coroner put down said Chrissie Watkins was high, drowned, and got cut up by a propeller. Levi concurred. A tragic accident. Real gross. Coroner made a joke about crabs, which confirmed my dislike for him. Chrissy was the niece of someone who owned *the* most prominent gift shop in town. They identified the poor girl not by her crowns, but by the little sand dollars etched into her bracelet.

My friend Josette said this was a bad omen. She was either going to leave or get rich by trading her pastoral marsh landscapes for repurposed disaster footage.

She said, "I can feel it. This particular summer we're inside right now is bearing darkness. All I'll have to do is wait. Then it's off to Provincetown."

I had only heard of the killer white from a class I took on larger terrestrial marine biology at Brown. They didn't seem like the kind of things to go after people. According to Levi, this wasn't the first attack. Only a few miles down the coast, about a month before Chrissy, an immigrant who worked at a Dock n' Dine restaurant went casting for stripers at high tide. Waist deep in the surf, his arm was torn clean off as if it had been attached to the elbow by red Velcro. He didn't make the papers. Cops blamed a bad marriage between tackle and the undertow.

The mayor was not happy: "I mean we sit around eating diner pad thai all winter until tourists flood the parking lots in late May and if they're not tan and wet, then they're not having a good time." The mayor said, "We gotta resolve the problem and get rid of the shark," without admitting there was a shark so I had to really think creatively. It's not easy to get rid of a pretend shark.

At a far booth of the Pancake Man Diner, I met with Cado, the mayor's assistant. "Alonzo. Find a way to get rid of the fish smell," he said.

I was not hungry as I could still taste the crab-eaten body in my nose hairs. I told him, "All right, I would think about how to do that. We all have something at stake here. It affects me personally seeing as how my cousin runs a petrol station in Hempstead. The only one before the ferry launch."

Cado told me this beach had been a cursed place forever. Its teenage keepers are out for blood, and they rove in packs at the first hint of warmth in the night. They are possessed by oyster slime mixed with dirty Sprite. In the morning, they've left triangles painted across billboards and have stolen whatever they can, leaving both tourist daughters and sons totally empty inside. Dig deep enough in the sand and you'll find what they've hidden there. A syringe or condom snakeskins packed with sickness from the Midwest. Dig deeper and the artifacts of another time will show themselves to you.

Even Ichabod quit using the beach for inspiration, instead choosing to stay inside and sketch made-up surfers. None of them had eyes.

I took a drive to my friend D'Eleanor's house. D'Eleanor and my old college friend Jem ran an ice cream shop by the boardwalk. I drove by the cottages and shack-to-mansions, which were all named things like Land's Edge, Stew's Paradise, or McMiller's Cove. They're all the same, each one filled with kids bored of their parent's drinking problems and defined solely by white furniture. My cousin's gas station sold maps that omitted these things.

D'Eleanor bought her parent's beach house just so she could tan naked on the roof. Her nest there became a guard post for spotting the shark's black spade. An oiled harpooner riding a cape-colonial. She told me I was getting lumpy. Vacation towns will do that. I opened all the windows to let in a bar band down the street while she displayed a barometer made from a balloon and a Smuckers jar. As we kissed on her couch, its upholstery turned from white to blue. She parted the buttons of my Hawaiian shirt like a surgeon creating a chest cavity from which to remove the heart and told me to shoot my jazz in between her back dimples. We ate kettle corn on the roof until it got cold out.

A week later it was a kid. A boy was eaten by this hypothetical fish smell right in front of the whole New London ferry while it unloaded morning day-trippers. That's how I knew the shark was a witch. Witches go for kids. The Portuguese started calling it Jesus. The drink filled with DIY farmer-tanned hunters. Filo's Gun Repair shop was able to branch out as a chain, just from upcharging the water logged rifle repairs.

Every tourist used a camera to permanently memorialize the scene: White caps like Styrofoam floating amongst gore. Mangled raft beyond the point of ever being patched or reinflated. A mother calling out her son's name. You can still find photographs in undeveloped Kodachrome baskets at antique shops. If developed, the photographs show clouds in the shapes of sea monsters. If you squint hard enough there are human remains crystallizing in the mud below.

"It's not readily apparent, but they're there. Trust me." Josette insisted this, keeping her hair away from the moisture in the air by gathering it in a bandana. By this point she reverted back to painting. With oil and horsehair she could control the past.

These shark-shaped clouds turned black. A depression skirted the coast until the sky ripped open and it poured for a week straight. D'Eleanor and Jem had forecasted this weeks prior and installed umbrellas outside of their ice cream shop. When the storm rolled away people would need to bathe. Ridding the grease from their interiors. That was it. Do something, we have to do something. Crosses, make more crosses. Pull the humid afternoon to all four corners and really mean it.

This was when the mayor himself asked me to do something, bypassing Cado. I had never actually met the mayor or seen the tiny anchors on his suit up close. I said okay, I'll do that Mayor because the money would be enough to actually get away from Amityville. The mayor and I shook hands on this and I smelled my hand later to find it minty.

When I'm at an impasse, I'd walk around the boardwalk with D'Eleanor and have a churro with extra mud and maybe a brewskie and think on it. Here the arcades were bursting at their seams. We danced to their music all the while being mocked by the tarot reader's electronic cackle. The Audubon Society was hired to bring in more gulls to clean up after the tourists. The gulls, however, attracted an infestation of raccoons after all the fowl eggs.

D'Eleanor's face, now tanned to rust, lit up with an idea. "Why don't we bait the shark with rare steaks?"

D'Eleanor didn't read the news. She didn't see how some fishermen from Austin caught a bull shark with a rib eye and hung their catch like a war criminal for all the papers. This was the incorrect killer. Its stomach flushed nothing but car parts when they sliced it open. I knew Jesus was smarter than to be caught with beef. Raccoons waited beneath us, flashing up their silver eyes. I looked over the water with the carousel grease and cinnamon in my throat and I knew what I had to do.

The phone rang five times on the line to my college friend Kirsten. 8 PM Long Island time, 10 PM Amazon time. Kirsten devoted her doctorate to studying in Porto de Madeira, planting tags in pink river dolphins. Last time we talked she bragged about how her team had been led by natives to a remote lagoon where they found something much better. Swamp apes. They lived in mud instead of trees. A museum in New Haven hired her to set up a breeding sanctuary for them.

Kirsten told me it wasn't that miraculous. "Mostly the gillmen sit around eating Tyson turkeys. That's their favorite. The matrons hunt."

Kirsten was going to use most of the grant to travel. To pay off student loans. Over the phone I recited my plan. I told her about the dead swimmers.

She said it was a stupid idea and I asked her to sleep on it. I called the same time next week and she had thought about it/was mad at New Haven/would consider it. The mayor was really breathing down my neck because Jesus had killed again. A marsh mucking New Yorker near the creek. "There's not gonna be a job for any of us next year if this shark keeps taking our tourists," the mayor told me with his hair flapping in the wind.

So Levi, Cado, and I left for Brazil. We ate yogurt on the plane. When we landed, we were greeted at customs by armed men screaming at an elderly couple with plaid legs. They were caught smuggling coolers stuffed with lobsters stuffed with cocaine. A homeless man freighting his balls in a wheelbarrow told me the flies here think you're already dead. The customs agents gave us a few lobsters as welcome gifts. Our van driver played a tape in his stereo that was only different versions of Elton John's 'Philadelphia Freedom.' Cado made him turn it down low enough where we couldn't hear it at all.

It was three hours of dirt road to camp. Kirsten fed us allspice loaves cooked right from the bark. Since college, Kirsten had shaken off the Katherine Hepburn lip we grew up with in Saybrook. She successfully became a new native Californian, speaking slower and standing with her arms always winged out as if her back bothered her. She carried around a blow dart gun on a sling that parted her in half.

"Don't talk to anyone," Kirsten said. "And lock your tent. It's eel mating season. They can traverse land."

"That's disgusting. How do you lock a tent?" She showed me how to do this, which involved fixing twine on the inside where the zipper meets the flap.

"When do I see the, you know."

"Be patient. She probably already sees you," Kirsten said. She fed us baby food mashed from rotten papaya. "This is mostly what we live off here."

Being in the jungle was a lot like living in a van that had been left in a hot parking lot. To the eyes it was a feast. The ferned edges of the lagoon exploded in toxic sherbet. The liquid at its core was still and black just like they say it is. All shitty with toucans. Cado took up trying to cook homemade toothpaste. Levi prodded the people on Kirsten's team with questions about football.

We cracked open the cocaine lobsters and became part of the forest. I forgot about Rhode Island and its horrible wide open views. There was no need for sunglasses. Here I was safe and confined to a mansion of forgotten about greenhouses. I could finally see the world for what it was.

Kirsten was going to sell us a mud gorilla for cheap. The mayor's office wired over more money than I cared to think about. According to her research, the young gillmatrons, because of their faster metabolism, were more likely to attack bait, whereas the mature specimens didn't get to it as fast.

"We need to preserve the younger gals. Give 'em a chance to grow. Normally they'd just live off water lily roots and small mammals, but now they're really getting a taste for the frozen chickens," Kirsten told us, fastening guts upon guts of rope. "It won't be hard to nab a grandmother though. I got one in mind. You'll see a tag tragus piercing right in her left ear."

Bait was laid out and the only thing to do was wait for one to surface. For hours we watched the oil. We saw as the poultry became orbited by light bulb sized greenflies. I imagined dropping a match into the lagoon and it going up in flames. Creating a symphony of car tire and gas station coffee. When it got dark and the eels began whistling, it meant it was the night's turn and the four of us retreated into separate tents.

The second morning I came to covered in moths. Kirsten had already gotten up, dressed, made papaya grinders, struck a gillmatron with a tranquilizer dart and wrapped it up like a mummy, all in dampened gauze. Her blow gun was bent in the scuffle. I didn't press. We were reprimanded by the rubber and hazelnut bearing boughs above. Thousands of undiscovered species watched us steal their queen away, getting louder. Warning: never come back!

We transported her on the bed of a truck, driving through the night to the airport. Kirsten's men crossed themselves whenever they caught sight of it, so I did too. They carried it like pallbearers to the back of a plane. I drank apple cider on the plane and ate BBQ almonds. My fingertips were sour and earthy which I worried might be a symptom of malaria. I forgot about this when we landed because as Levi says, this is the part where God has stopped speaking to you.

The mayor sent a U-Haul for us, packed with ice we didn't need. I had to put my sunglasses back on to defend myself against the horizon. We removed our gillmatron's wrapping. We saw in the dark that she was flabby and her face sagged with cheek bladders. Her body was covered by patchy cinnamon fur in some places and by scale in others. Kirsten concluded the mud apes had layers of blubber in order to keep them warm in deep water.

Levi volunteered to shoot ketamine into her armpit fins because he had a daughter who was allergic to wasps and he was well practiced in stabbing needles. Cado lit sage either to cover the hot pond smell, or to absolve us of the act of robbing a tropical place. In the truck we didn't talk about anything much. Just hummed our gillmatron a Skynyrd B-side she probably never heard before.

Back on the peninsula, we returned to our anchors. Levi, a belt radio. Cado, to his dental floss. For me it was wayfarers with extra dense pillars. The kind an old timer with cataracts would sport. I trimmed the lice outta my sideburns. My landlord had repainted the cement of our patio. Ichabod rolled his ankle on it which forced him to draw while hunched in a chair. His sketches only showed waves with surfers that were insinuated.

D'Eleanor and I lied to one another about how we spent the last couple weeks, and chose to believe one another's fables. We had sex in her car and ate cheeseburgers from a gray McDonalds that looked like it was part of the boardwalk. It was cold when we woke up which reminded us of Thanksgiving time and the cul-de-sacs we were born on.

The gillmatron was dying from inside the U-Haul, trapped in a tank normally reserved to transport carp to Chinese buffets and koi pond wholesalers. We parked her behind the marina. They paid guys to keep a steady flood of ketamine and ice going into her as if she were a weird case of brewskies. She spent every night chirping. There was nothing outside the U-Haul to respond. I was worried she wouldn't last long enough to make it out to sea.

On Monday as soon as the weekenders left we made our move. We got up before daybreak and brought the truck to the launch. On the jetty was a new cross dressed in flower leis. Someone who drowned naturally, who will be forgotten because he did not die spectacularly in the midst of violence. Taped to the cross was a yearbook photo of him. A man with crow feather hair and a smile which made him seem like he had fewer teeth than a regular person, though I figured it was bad luck to chastise the dead. We could see our breath, it was so freezing. I saw a horseshoe crab beach itself. Bad luck, according to Cado. I said I'd stay behind and return the truck.

"You're going out with us," Cado said. "We're finishing this together." Levi did not come to my defense. He plugged his ears to mask the truck's beeping. When I lifted the gate we were thrown back, gagging, by fetid pond humidity.

"She reeks."

"You would too if you were in that situation," Levi said.

"Let's get this over with."

They brought both me and the gillmatron, unwilling, to a small boat. Its engine was a sad thing, bitter at having to accommodate passengers. It sputtered out a glaze of gasoline behind us.

That was my first time ever being on the drink. I should've worn two pairs of sunglasses because all around I was swallowed by space with nothing to shield me. It was close to when the seals would come out. This made our presence all the more dangerous. Levi said Jesus wasn't after seals. It only had eyes for men.

We propped the gillmatron up. She was awake but slow to move. Hands and snout banded like lobsters before you drop 'em in the pot. Cado sliced one band from the body. She studied Cado with deeply set cue balls. I hacked the other band off, grazing rattlesnake boot skin. She unfolded on the starboard, taller than any of us. She was hissing and making cricket noises and this sounded like it was coming from us and not her. I thought maybe she would kill me then so I closed my eyes to ready myself but there was a splash. We were left in the engine's flatulence. Our own scum.

On the ocean the ripples calmed and I saw how the papaya had shaped my face and finished me in washed copper. Things felt ok then. Sometimes things feel ok, though who among us has time to watch themselves in oceans?

Go get him. Get that shark, we sang. We returned to land and I used my switcher knife to cut a popsicle off its stick into a bowl which I ate while listening to the radio. I wished Josette was around to paint me but she was already on the way to Provincetown.

I celebrated with Ichabod, eating milkshakes made from Oreos that lodged themselves in the straw.

In a week our shark was blown up by some cowboys in a fishing boat, way out deep under shooting meteor stars. The mayor's money became a coat to keep me intact. Kirsten told me the dolphins left to breed in flood season beds upriver. The mud apes, too encased in blubber to float, became frightened of humans and her grant was revoked.

Over brownie bottom sundaes at Jem's, I was passed a rumor from a local oyster farmer. He claimed the shark was summoned not by accident, but by a roving pack of witches. Our shooter on the grassy knoll theory.

"These witches were descendants from Massachusetts who learned to never settle. They have a van. I've seen it," the farmer said. We ignored him until he wandered off and then Jem brought us three more brownie bottom sundaes.

We swept the beach out of the businesses. It got tracked back in. Ichabod fell in love with one of his invisible surfers. What had been a great white of winter and animal came to blur together. My widowed gulls kept in circles, gabbing. *Come back to us.*

Little by little, sand gets trapped in crevices. It builds up and no one has the gumption to get in there and deep clean. More New Londoners arrive and leave by the ferry. More kids of tourists have bonfires to set up stories about the kids who died before them, except the stories change. They morph a little more out of proportion each year with little details that corrupt the larger ones. In an effort to dispel bad juju they rename the ferries the Nina, Pinta, and Santa Marino after Dan Marino.

Elton John will not reveal in interviews whether the lyrics of 'Can You Feel the Love Tonight' are actually an incantation that attracts great whites. I tell this to D'Eleanor at the Pancake Man.

"Take off those stupid sunglasses," D'Eleanor says. "You look fucking dumb." At this moment it is the kind of moment I think we could settle down. She is so tan I can smell how her moles have been fried.

In winter I sit in our karaoke bar with Levi and Ichabod eating hot dogs in lobster roll buns. Levi yells about a story he read in the paper about how March snow disturbed the dunes. Decimated the wooden stairways where people once plodded down in bare feet. This is when all kinds of debris will wash up. According to the paper, an old timer walking his dog found something all adorned in sea and weed like a debutante. Not really a person. Not really a fish. Some in-between thing that was never fully one or the other and after it was dead, no one knew where to bury it.

D'Eleanor died from melanoma that spread like Pacific wildfire in her chest. Josette went missing on her way to the fist of Cape Cop. Abandoned all her paintings and photographs. According to Cado, Josette was the shark's final victim. He says it takes the form of anything. Trees, pills, men, whatever. Leaving nothing but slime trails and limbs.

When the ground unthawed, we held a metaphorical funeral behind Captain's Cove mini golf park for the gillmatron and D'Eleanor. Levi propped up a toy lighthouse as a marker. With swooped bangs tickling his eyeballs, he sang Skynyrd to our loved ones. A Dollar Store siren. We were all letting our hair grow out to obscure our faces as something we could hide behind. Even Ichabod, hunchbacked and balding, wore a brilliant crown of hay.

Jem bowed her head and said, "It was a love spell. The fish grew in us like watermelon seeds do. A vine that curls in your tum-tum, eventually snaking out and forcing you to speak with an accent that seemed to come from out of nowhere. You have to do something about this or it'll find someone else to settle down with." She didn't look at me, though it was obvious. Cado said a prayer in Portuguese and then left for New Bedford and never came back.

Inside sticky half mornings I'll hear another generation howling at the sides of their bonfires, where they conjure their own story. Repurposing antiques into sequels. Evil passing like spit while youth burns whatever the ocean sends back. Amityville's fateful step-summer changes its shape with every year. In one version, Jesus swam up the creek and swallowed an inner tube. In another version its teeth are yellow and the hippy girl is still alive in its stomach. Both of them swimming around like that forever.

500 million years

Bentgrass generates dense turf with a fine texture, making it ideal for golf courses. It can be mowed as short as one-tenth of an inch. Keep in mind, bentgrass needs regular watering. It thrives in the humid climates of the northeastern United States, as drought, excess shade, insects, disease, and warmer temperatures can create hostile conditions. Due to the high cost of fungicides, insecticides, fertilizer, and mowing tools required to maintain a bentgrass lawn at home, it is rarely selected by families.

"This is what we're doing. We're gonna go to Boca Laredo, and make a sandcastle," says the neckbeard in Orlando Magic sweatpants.

Tortilla chips, soft with guacamole runoff, spill from my mouth.

"How big?" I ask, half-crying.

Neckbeard holds his hands apart from each other to indicate approximately two feet. 500 million years in slug time.

"No, no way, we're not doing that," I say.

Dueling flamenco guitar solos wail over maracas and a trumpet somewhere in the background. Neckbeard surveys the cantina and asks where all the cactus paintings went. I tell him something about democracy and it's all over.

Earlier, we'd been down in Arkansas selling Snail Honey. Except Neckbeard called it 'Our Kansas' and I decided quickly not to correct him. We packaged the honey in empty pine nut jars and sold them for ten dollars. When a customer would furrow their brow in question of where exactly the snail came in, I'd explain how our honey isn't honey, but rather enzymatic nectar repurposed from grass-fed, soft-boiled mollusks, that fermented in repurposed pomegranate juice barrels into a bone-fortifying amino-B4-enriched product that's been proven to alleviate joint pain, fatigue, and cellulite. We don't tell customers the stuff actually originates from a BPA-infested plastic bottle shaped like a bear, prior to being sealed in jars we rinsed out in a Safeway bathroom.

Life was hard on the road for my compadres and I. Our '96 Chevy Express was filled to the brim with boxes of Snail Honey, and I couldn't tell if the rattling sound above 65 mph was the jars clanking together or the catalytic converter trying to fall off. But I would say the thick of our adventure started on a day in a desert that used to be a cornfield.

"At least, I think there used to be cornfields here," Dr. Billclinton tells me, and I suspect Neckbeard hears too. Dr. Billclinton is an agrologist. This means she studies grass. Seeds, lawns, fields, fronds, you name it. Professionally, she does it to further advance the technology of lawn care. On a personal level, she respects grass for its all-encompassing importance to mankind. I don't say it out loud, but I do think I'm in love with her. I have a plan to tell her this when the moment sits right because there's a certain moment for everything if you can wait long enough for it.

Before all this, I had plans to dig myself a hole in the gem-encrusted Australian countryside. Australia is among the world's safest nations. Doors are sold without locks there. I'd find me one of those blonde ladies and start a co-op farm to grow weed and pumpkins and dingoes. I told acquaintances I didn't care how tough the Outback soil was. They'd warn me that there's more to that country than Outbacks and dingoes. There is more to life than Outbacks and dingoes (yeah, right). But then, Dr. Billclinton enters. My almost-wife, except she's already been to Australia. She grew up there.

The three of us stand inside the vestibule of an Arizonian diner. A bolts-and-vinyl satellite baking in a squishy parking lot with bear grass jutting out from its cracks. A waitress with a *Halle* name tag semi-politely informs us we can seat ourselves. Neckbeard sits beside Dr. Billclinton in the booth and I get my own little area. The doctor plays with the duct tape holding the vinyl together while I thumb through the tabletop jukebox. Neckbeard asks if they've got any Batch.

"It's pronounced Bash," I correct him.

"What did I say?" Neckbeard mutters, but he's transfixed on the menu. I know for sure I'm getting Snickers pancakes, but I read the full menu anyway, seeing as how the jukebox was just for show and the buttons are frozen solid. Beyond the window the sun is white and wavy, just the way I like it. The greenhouse effect is in full swing with heat breathing through glass to keep everyone's eggs warm.

The waitress makes her way to us and pours coffee into glossy brown mugs.

"Hey, do you have anyone soilating the xerophyllum in the parking lot?" Dr. Billclinton asks. Halle is fifty-eight or an unhealthy forty-five. She has cigarette fingers and smells like the color mauve. Her uniform matches the picture of the French toast sundae on the very last page of the menu.

I grunt a polite laugh to alleviate Halle's discomfort. "Excuse me. The bear grass. It's a predatory perennial to the fig population," Dr. Billclinton says.

"You mean the plants are a threat to the bugs?" Halle says. She does not look pleased. The doctor hands over her menu.

"Figs aren't insects. They're a breed of sparrow." Even I didn't know that.

Our food comes out full of Halle's spit. Napkins are scrunched into balls. Jelly packets are scraped clean. I'm only able to finish three pancakes. We rehash our business plan. I can tell the families herding in are coming from church by all their bleach knee denim. They bottleneck next to the dessert spinner, scowling at us. The husbands don't like how we're holding our office meeting in their seats.

"I got this one. I'll meet you guys by the van," the doctor says.

Neckbeard and I let our farts out in the parking lot, but also a little by the waiting families. I walk around, picking pieces of pancake meat from my molars, careful not to disturb the grass. When the doctor catches up to us, Neckbeard asks her about her necklace, and she makes up a story about her grandmother passing it down through the generations because she made it through some historic blimp fire in the 1930s. The doctor's cheek has hot sauce or ketchup on it that she is trying to lick off.

I pivot on my heels.

"Hold on. My leftovers." I start to head back but Dr. Billclinton throws her arm against my chest and tells me to forget it. "I have a whole second breakfast in there," I say.

"There's nothing for you in there but processed sugar," she says, jabbing my stomach with the keys. This brings a laugh out of Neckbeard, even though he's over forty pounds overweight. Maybe the doctor is right. I abandon my Snicker pancakes and follow my compadres into our van heavy with slug oil.

The afternoon sets and rises a few times. Political election coverage entertains the three of us on motel TVs. These big, navy blue storm clouds form in our wake, but we point the van towards the sun. We've added a thousand miles to the odometer driving to some town the doctor swears will be a lucrative venture. Neckbeard is asleep in the back. The check engine light is on and I'm less than optimistic about passing emissions.

"Not in Arizona," Dr. Billclinton tells me. She sits too close to the dashboard. Her arms vibrate against the freeway construction's washboard asphalt. "They don't do emission testing out here. We're in the Wild West of automotive pollution."

We bought the van, used, from a lot at three in the morning. There were three cassette tapes under the shotgun seat. One was nothing but soothing ocean sounds, with whales on the reverse side. The other two tapes were the soundtracks to Disney movies. Dr. Billclinton snapped the radio antennae off to toast marshmallows over a small brush fire we made on a trail overlooking the freeway one night. It feels like home only when we cover the floor mats with drive-thru fries and coffee cups. Neckbeard tapes burger wrappers over the rear windows to make curtains. I ask if we're there yet, and instead of laughing the doctor says,

"That's funny." She rolls the window down to wind whipping at her ponytail. I try to fall asleep in my seat with fabric that reeks of 7UP. I imagine Dr. Billclinton and I holding hands, riding on the backs of mermaids covered in soft koala fur that moves like wind over wheat. I try imagining her without a ponytail and glasses, but it's difficult and the ocean tastes too much like a soda.

"Lawrence, wake up!" Neckbeard is shaking me. "We're here!"

"In-where-in?" My nose is unbelievably itchy. I can hear Dr. Billclinton knocking crates of Snail Honey from the back of the van.

"Welcome to Greenlee," the doctor exclaims with open arms. Greenlee is a place I can feel in my lungs, almost immediately. The air swarms in the eye of a pine storm. But all I can see is metal. Chicken wing palaces. Traffic warnings flashing like broken alarm clocks.

"Look," Neckbeard whispers, signaling to a distant mountain. "Incredible."

I've never in my life seen so many houses packed together, the same peach color with the same tile roofs. Both of us are mesmerized at how the glimmer of swimming pools shoots afternoon stars across the mountain. Neckbeard tells me he wants to live there someday. I tell him we'll have to wait and see.

The doctor hands me a crate. She leads us around a building into a clearing.

"Astroturf," she says. She puts her finger in her mouth like she's trying to gag.

"Everyone's wearing hats." Neckbeard frowns.

"Welcome to the Greenlee Sunday Farmer's Market," Dr. Billclinton says. She opens our table with two direct kicks to the legs. The three of us stand side by side by side. Our banner hangs beneath samples that we've spread on a picnic blanket with a grass stain the doctor covered with a ceramic snail. The holes we hide with pamphlets illustrated by Neckbeard's hand drawn bumblebees.

Everyone else has a fancy collapsible tent. We look like idiots without one. I think about stealing someone else's tent as I stroll by tomatoes like shiny green human hearts, corn, pesto, and bread with oats baked on top. Trout caught just yesterday, displayed over ice that the doctor puts in her coffee. All of it spills from tote bags lugged by parents with sweater ponchos and kids on leashes chasing labs on leashes.

People avoid eye contact with us. As the afternoon heats up, the stink of the fish is no longer masked by handmade soaps and pies. An old lady with sunglasses covering her entire face ambles up. I can feel Neckbeard's fear.

"Good morning," Dr. Billclinton says in her most enthusiastic voice. The lady asks about the honey and I tell her all about it. I tell her what the doctor told me, some time ago at a truck stop four hundred miles away:

Neckbeard and I were on a reverse road trip back from a potential job in New Mexico, or Old Mexico, or one of the Mexico's, transporting thousands of dollars in Walmart gift cards. Needless to say, we were under-qualified, and were drowning our sorrows with soft drinks in a parking lot when this girl asks us if our truck needs a jump. She's got this razor-sharp ponytail and thick eyeglass frames with thin lenses. She's short but stands with her arms on the hips of her khaki shorts in this weird power stance that makes her look taller. I tell her we appreciate it but don't need a jump. Then she asks our names and I am thinking holy crap.

The part where she said we needed a bigger car if we wanted to sell Snail Honey came after the part where she told us about how much money there was to be made from Snail Honey. We were sitting at a picnic table. She used a pen that said Flagstaff Sheriff's Department on it in gold foil, which she put to her arm and wrote: Young urban professionals + influx of entry-level campaign management positions in Southwest Arizona + agro-tourism + pomegranate + fair-trade + Organic = $$$, with a smiley face. Except she draws the smiley face on the top of my hand and I feel the ball of the pen gliding on my skin and her eyes meet mine and I am like *holy effin crap*.

I watch Dr. Billclinton take a twenty from the lady. The doctor thanks her with this smile that turns her into a person I haven't met yet. She does this at least forty or fifty more times that day. Neckbeard and I sit in folding chairs and just kind of take it in until the sky gets all pink and oily. We start packing up. When I lift the cigar box it weighs about as much as a coffee table book about canyons. The doctor says her migraines are back but you'd never know because we're laughing in the van above the cassette deck as loud as it goes. I'm driving while Neckbeard is in the front seat. The doctor counts money in the back, singing along to the song. It's something about the Fourth of July and for a moment I get this feeling like we're a family. Mr. and Mrs. Billclinton hyphenated with my last name because I consider myself an upwardly mobile professional for the time being.

"There!" The doctor points to an Applebee's. We order apple crisp sundaes for dinner and they come out still cooking on an iron skillet that fills the bar with smoke. I look around at all the other families and office workers and we are no different. I see the doctor's grin through the bottom of my oversized mug. For a second it looks like she's missing a tooth. I tell her she looks familiar, but I'm drunk and I tell her this in a way where all the words are connected.

"I got the bill. You guys warm up the van," she says.

Outside, the smoke from the vents is scorched peppers. I have cinnamon from the apple crisp on my tongue. We pull out of the parking lot, right on red. The doctor's driving. I have no idea where we are going, but I don't care. It's freezing out so we drive with the heat on. Neckbeard is asleep in the back. Three cop cars with blaring Christmas decorations speed by. All the other white, green, and blue lights from gas stations join to dance on the smudges across our windshield. We pull over for an ambulance. I think about the future and the cigar box getting heavier, and having to buy more cigar boxes. With us joining the highway I try picking the apple peels out from in between my teeth in case me and Dr. Billclinton start kissing. It could be any highway. The peppers stay in our clothes even as we step outside before a Super 8 with free HBO.

Bermuda grass is an excellent choice for a residential lawn because it can withstand low mowing heights. It spreads by stolons and rhizomes, forming a thick, dense grass as a result. It's native to the South, though can be found as far north as Kansas. Bermuda grass upkeep requires rigorous fertilizing, watering, and mowing. Early summer is the optimum time to plant Bermuda grass, when the soil has warmed up and the threat of spring frost has passed.

The TV is stuck on the nature channel. Neckbeard falls asleep again fast on a cot the doctor found in the closet. I'm lying in the twin-sized bed when Dr. Billclinton emerges from the bathroom wearing only her shorts and the same facial expression she has when she counts money. I pretend to watch a documentary about seagulls but I can see tan lines on boobs jumping in my periphery as she slides into the bed. When she doesn't use a pillow as a barricade I think something is going to happen and it sobers me up all too quickly. She takes my hand and leaves it on her stomach. I don't talk, I just listen so close that the sound of the seagulls completely falls off.

"Remember those Magic Eye books? When I was a kid those books were all everyone cared about," she says. "You had them too, right? My brothers were so good at finding the white tigers and pyramids that I, no matter what, could never see. After they went to sleep, I'd lie on the lemon clover in the backyard with a lighter and stare into the pages. I'd be out there in the cold for hours. You know, lemon clover is edible. But too much can almost kill you. A little messes with your brain, but in a good way. It proves how warm the Milky Way is."

People are arguing in the parking lot. A couple from the sound of it. I'm glad we pulled the curtains shut. They have no idea what's happening in here.

"I stayed out there so late one night I got pneumonia," Dr. Billclinton says.

"That's serious," I say. It's the only thing I can think to say because she is not making sense.

"It is," she says. "I gave it to my grandma too. Don't worry though, that's not what cut her down." She stops and turns her head on the pillow's dust. I swallow a pepper-onion burp. "Someday. Someday we're going to have a farm there. We're going to raise dingoes and have pumpkins as pets," she says.

"What do pumpkins eat?" I croak, trying desperately not to wake Neckbeard. Just in case. I think about trying to kiss her face. The arguing outside has turned to one voice. A car peels out.

"It's Atalanta. My name," she says before falling asleep.

Goodnight, Atalanta, I think I say out loud, but I cannot confirm this.

For such a cold night, the morning air is a stagnant eighty-two degrees. I ask the doctor if Snail Honey needs to be kept chilled, and she says it's fine and to just get in the van.

"My head is fucking killing me," she says.

"Lucky for you I always carry Tylenol. Extra strength rapid dissolve." I have three capsules in my palm ready to go, proud of how swiftly I produce them.

"Tylenol makes my pee burn. Thank you though, Lair, you're too sweet."

At McDonald's I put fountain Coke in our iced coffees just the way we like them. Neckbeard yawns into his and Dr. Billclinton blesses him. She tells this story about how back home the old folks would say 'God bless you' when people yawned, because Tasmanian phantoms would drown you in the ocean if your yawn wasn't properly blessed. Neckbeard doesn't buy it. He draws a picture of the van on a Texas Gulf map from our glove box.

And so we drive our fan full of honey down interstates. I can't tell if we're leaving a trail of billowing black air or if we're chasing one. Farmer's market after motel after farmer's market after motel after farmer's market. Some markets have pastries baked with herbs you wouldn't think are good, but would be surprised. Some motels have framed photographs of dogs hanging in their lobby that you can pull off the wall without anyone yelling at you.

We make enough money for wicker baskets. We're halfway across Oklahoma when we've made enough money to buy a change of clothes. Dr.

Billclinton gets this shirt with the silhouette of a bear on it and I buy the kind of hat a fisherman would wear. We take a sharp right in Arkansas, when we get to an accident and there's a roadblock.

"Muggy out today," I tell the doctor. We're at our table, and we've made enough money for professional signage. We pack up and pile into the van for what feels like the thirtieth time. We've all memorized the words to the songs on the cassette tapes, and we've gotten tired of singing them. It never occurs to me we could buy new tapes, but we've made enough money —

— "to buy a gun," Dr. Billclinton states.

"We don't need a gun. Why do we need a gun?" I ask her.

"Fine, no gun," she says, immediately turning away. We're loading the van. We've mastered the skill of peeling tiny neon price stickers from jars without leaving residue. We've even made enough money to print off expensive looking labels at Staples, complete with the image of a riverside barn and words like 'tradition' and 'superfood.' We rebrand as *snailhoney*.

We're in Texas, I think. Our booth is the fanciest of all the booths, and there's gotta be at least forty or fifty vendors here. Neckbeard says it's the Mall of America of farmer's markets. We're adjacent to another honey stand and Neckbeard flips them off, but I slap his hand down before anyone sees. A woman running for senator will be driving by later and there are a fuck ton of yard signs with her last name on them. The doctor says the metal used in sign posts poisons the grass and this entire field will be dead in three hundred years.

"It's called Horticultural Alzheimer's. The aluminum makes the grass forget how to be grass."

These two young guys walk up to our table and one wearing sunglasses picks up a pamphlet. I tell Neckbeard as quietly as I can that it's Jonathan Taylor Thomas' brother.

"Snails, eh?" One says to the other. Or us, I can't tell. I start telling them about the antioxidants and how it helps regenerate cells absolutely vital for muscle growth. He watches me while chewing on apple skin.

"Why's a snail farm have a mill? This real?" The boy without sunglasses says this, looking at our new logo on Dr. Billclinton's chest. She folds her arms and asks if they would be interested in reversing the dangerous effects of air pollution.

"Does she come with the honey," the boy with sunglasses says. We all laugh.

"It's all in this little jar of miracles," the doctor recites.

"I've heard good things about this snail honey. Real solid stuff," sunglasses says.

"Is there a bulk discount?" No Sunglasses folds his arms too, so the muscles twitch. "What if I buy a whole case? Would you come hang out for a while? We have a sailboat. A thirty-footer." The other one laughs, somehow without smiling.

"Thanks, you guys," she says through clenched teeth. "Have a good one."

"I can tell how beautiful you are under all that hippy shit," sunglasses says, so close I can taste the mint on his breath. He rests his hands on our booth, wrinkling the tablecloth. "And you know, I bet you smell like patchouli everywhere." Around us there is an enormous sky with one tiny cloud directly behind the boys' heads.

"Thank you." I can hear tears stab Dr. Billclinton's voice. I want to do something brave, but freeze up, even as I can feel hot adrenaline in my teeth. Neckbeard is stuck to his chair, silent and terrified.

"Fuck her and her fat hillbilly fuck-buddies. Let's grab that squash for D-rod and get down to the lake." Sunglasses swipes a jar of honey and they walk away real slow like they don't think I'm going to knock their lights out. I can't look at the doctor. I tell her I was going to fight them off but I know she doesn't believe me. She walks away and I get this feeling like she's never coming back. I think about how much I would miss her as she disappears into the parking lot with our blanket under her arm.

Dichondra is typically found in California and Arizona. It is common in residential lawns since it can be mowed to create a dense, attractive turf. Along its creeping stems, leaves tend to fan in opposite directions. Dichondra necessitates a steady supply of fertilizer and is susceptible to insects and diseases. Dichondra is best suited for tiny areas rather than vast lawns or regions where mowing proves difficult, as it does not tolerate excessive traffic. Invasions of broadleaf weeds are prevalent and difficult to keep under control.

We're driving down the Texas coastline in the Chevy Express. Dr. Billclinton tells me we're not stopping until we get to the southernmost tip of Central America. We start stashing the money in empty snailhoney crates. Big wads of cash held tight with the infinite supply of hair elastics in the doctor's pocket. I am beginning to think her ponytail is permanent.

Sometimes when I'm driving down an endless stretch of interstate and 'A Whole New World' comes on from the kids' movie cassette tape, I think of this one time the doctor's glasses slid down her nose and I saw her eyes, like iguana scales outlined in crusty black warrior paint. Literally. We made enough money to buy a novelty tin of warrior face paint. At that moment there was nothing separating her eyes from mine, and I grin this massive grin when I think of this.

We make enough money to buy suits and briefcases. We make enough money to bury in ditches off the road. We mark the ditches with small crosses. We sell twelve crates of snailhoney to an organic grocery chain forager. We've made too much money and Neckbeard is crowded in the backseat with shopping bags full of cash that he uses as a pillow. The three of us are speeding down the highway, listening to a song without drums, about California when Neckbeard says,

"You know, this is just like that show. Two guys a girl and a pizza pl —"

The bottom of the van drops out. Neckbeard's head slams into the roof. The doctor jerks the wheel towards the shoulder, and I see thick sparks on dust in the rearview. I ask Neckbeard if he's alright, as Dr. Billclinton hops from her seat. We inspect the damage, swatting at smoke plumes. There's a cancerous plastic smell.

"We're fucking outta here." She hurls a shopping bag heavy with money into my chest.

"What?"

This guy behind us is on his car phone. He asks if we're okay, and says the entire muffler just fell off our van.

"Let's go," the doctor orders. It's starting to thunder. I notice it's the first time I've seen a storm in weeks. The clouds. I saw the clouds. Big dark ones, but they were behind us the whole time. Neckbeard looks up at the sky the way a child would to drink raindrops. We walk down the onramp, shopping bags slung over our backs. Away from the cold Chevy corpse. Rain turning several weeks' worth of dust into mud.

When we get to the Mexican restaurant there is someone who looks like they want to sell me a used Mercedes, wearing an apron and keeping their cigarette dry under an awning strung with cactus-shaped Christmas lights. He opens the door for us. We seat ourselves at the bar. My suit is dripping dye all over everything. The doctor tells me to order her whatever while she heads for the bathroom. I know I've arrived at the moment to tell her that I'm totally in love. I'm pretty sure she's going to say the same thing back to me, and our eyes are going to sting at the same time. I nudge the money under my stool, taking a good look around to make sure none of these people are thinking about stealing our luggage. In a commercial on the bar's TV, the woman running for senator shakes hands with children. It returns to the evening news. They're talking about the rainstorm. An end to a drought. There's a piece of paper taped to the bottom of the screen that says DO NOT PRESS MY BUTTONS.

"I don't know what we're doing," I say to Neckbeard, shoveling the free tortilla chips into my mouth.

I glance up from the salsa and I see her, pretty as she was when her glasses slid down her face. Except her hair isn't in a ponytail and she's on TV. Halle is on TV. Out of her apron, smiling in a Christmas sweater next to a guy wearing a US Navy hat. The bartender places three watermelon margaritas in front of me. The guys from the market are on the screen. Graduation gowns on. Little League photos. One of them was found in a blanket. Other people I've never met. There's a cop. All of them were initially thought to have suffered strokes until medical examiners realized the blood spatters inside the victims' skulls had all splattered in the exact shape as the state of Florida. There's a phone number. She's unarmed yet extremely dangerous. There's a reward. All I hear is Mariachi music.

It's easy to remember us back in the motel bed. I think of all the times talking in the van just to stay awake. That first time, when I told her about Australia and she said, "No way, I grew up there!" This big, surprised smile across her face. Going on about all the palm trees, she told me she lost her accent. The TV goes to commercial. Neckbeard tells me about sandcastles. I say something about democracy and the back of my throat hurts from swallowing sobs.

Dr. Atalanta Billclinton joins me at the bar. She tells me she's been starving. I ask why she needed to kill those people. If she was planning on killing us, too. She hesitates before slurping from the froth of her drink.

"Larry, there's too much you don't get about the world." She takes another sip, making sure to avoid the salt. I see this from the corner of my eye; at first I can't make my head turn to see her. "Do you think anything we've been doing is ethical? We're just the fang that makes the snake oil." Her voice sounds detached but I can still see that beautiful grass scientist squinting in the sun by a former cornfield.

"I know you, though. I know you," is what I tell her.

"I was raised by bears," she says. "In a black, black forest."

"We never even got to the part with the credit card scam and the co-op farm. The bronze in the Outback and the single-engine airplane that sounds like a bathroom fan about to break apart and catch all its dust on fire," I say, without knowing what I mean. I pick up two of the three shopping bags. People in the bar are staring now. Mumbling at each other about the girl from TV. The one from the rich family who went crazy. The one with the power to put gravel inside other people's brains.

"Come on," I say to Neckbeard. The doctor gives me this little nod. I don't remember who looked away first, but I know it was a while until one of us did.

Tall fescue is a cool-season grass that can also survive in southern climates due to its heat tolerance. It's a subtype of bunchgrass, commonly used on athletic fields for its ability to endure extensive tread and abuse. Patches of tall fescue may rise from some lawns, appearing as a grassy weed. Because it grows in clusters, it's rarely included in seed medleys. Tall fescue is a robust grass ideal for playgrounds. During winter, these grasses thrive in regions too hot for cool grasses but too cold for warm-season grasses.

The two of us are walking in spit rain with thousands of dollars in shopping bags. Neckbeard says he knew what she was doing, and I immediately forgive him. He says he knew how much I liked her.

"Do you think she liked me?" I ask. The bag is getting heavy fast.

"I don't know," Neckbeard tells me. "Life seems sort of backwards."

Tex-Mex music is stuck in my head. Grass scientists. Dingoes howling to the soundtrack of *Aladdin*. An infinite variety of squash floating up toward the Milky Way galaxy. Check engine lights trying to warn me of something obvious. Waitresses and kids with grieving families. Apples on a hot skillet. Big piles of pine nuts, discarded. Stuck in my head.

"Yeah. I guess life is pretty backwards sometimes. But you know, it feels like there would be a Walmart up this road."

THE WRECK

The Wreck is an Airbnb made from recovered barn timber and on the side "The Wreck" was once written in paintbrush. Randy did it with his nephew's art supplies, wearing the same Nike gym shorts, Adidas flip-flops and Under Armour shirt he wears when he is changing the door code or putting a band-aid over what's been broken. That is unless we see one another at St. John's Episcopal Church, in which case he'll be swimming in a royal blue button-down. Everything here, every piece of furniture, is permanently soaked in suntan lotion.

A layer of Feldspar Gray and one of Dovetail covers a urine stain if it stays in direct sunlight long enough. Each knock of the rubber mallet against the paint can lid sprays a little bit on my legs and sandals. My ability to renew normal wear and tear is, in my opinion, underestimated. Usually repainting isn't necessary, but in cleaning up after our most recent guests, I found that someone has definitely peed all over the siding. I can tell by the chemical odor and how the grass is still sticky. This strikes me as odd because why couldn't they have just gone in the outdoor shower or the herb garden? It's also odd, with them having all been women, how someone managed to direct their pee stream onto the house. The strangest thing is how the stream was acidic enough to remove a little of the original exterior color, but there's really no point in investigating because even with quick-dry paint, it will have barely set by the time our new guests arrive.

Once last summer, Randy wore a pink polo shirt and cargo shorts and his Adidas sandals while proving the space to a representative from Airbnb. That meeting ended in a whisper fight on the front lawn, which now looks a lot like hyena fur and is too sharp on bare feet. *The Wreck* was named after a real wreck in the cove. Technically, the cove is just an extension of the marsh. They say the marsh is dying and it smells like it, too. Someday its death will reach the cove, or it'll make its way up the creek to the start of the cottages, where my busted Nissan is parked right now with three Dunkin' cold brews scattered throughout its cup holders. Maybe the marsh's death won't stop there.

In the event our Lord is watching, I make sure to leave out a bowl of something like shells or candy or buttons after each mess is resolved. I put a potted palm tree in front of the urine stain. It's still showing through a little. Our new guests will arrive at noon. That gives me only one hour to bring *The Wreck* back to how she looks online in the photos. Seductive wood surfaces. Quirky furniture picked up from flea markets.

We're expecting a group of lady business professionals on a wellness retreat, which strikes me as odd because usually these types stay at the inns closer to town. They'll pay attention to how clean it is here. They'll most likely write a lengthy review. Randy tells me the itinerary sometimes so we know which canvas print to hang above the sofa in the common space. Depending on who's staying here, we'll change it between a black and white photograph of a yak with bangs, a rainy city street in Paris, Jimi Hendrix in drooling watercolors, sunflowers, or a Matisse rip-off of a woman smoking a long cigar. Each print appeals to a different psychology in our guests.

On my way to *The Wreck*, the cars on 6A were backed up halfway to Shanucket because a Peter Pan bus caught fire. Each passerby was forced to witness how the bus's engine had erupted in oil and tar and brimstone. I prayed for the people on the bus. All of them had gathered around where they could've been broiled alive moments before. I prayed that I could've left out a bowl of shells for them.

How the Lord tests the shoreline rental industry also happens to be our lifeblood. Sand. For that, I start with a slightly dampened mop, and once the floor is dry, I hand sweep the rest. Doesn't stop those crystals from scratching up the wood or chewing my carpets, but it helps. No matter how many times I chase the sand away, it always comes back.

In the late winter, when the beaches must be renewed, our motel parking lots fill with contracted dredging crews. Their machinery works to pull fresh sand from beneath the tide to deposit back on shore. When spring comes, the contractors are found in their rooms beneath piles of Keystone Light and breakfast sandwich wrappers.

Just as I finally got free of the traffic, the side street to the cottages was flooded again. This is because the marsh spews back rain if it gets even the slightest bit full. Like an idiot, I drove my Nissan right through it and now my Nissan makes an *urrturrgrbt* sound. After such a poor season, I cannot afford another car. Every other weekend a washout. The rain was so bad and the flies loved the floods. They fed on anyone stupid enough to pass through them, including me.

For today we've left up the yak.

The whispered argument Randy had with the Airbnb consultant and her clipboard was over Aspergillus mold in the basement and the pipes that burst in the outdoor shower. Randy was on the hunt for Mrs. Right. When his girlfriend broke up with him last spring, I saw his truck in the driveway for about two straight weeks. We lost thousands of dollars while he grieved. He told me he was finally fixing the rear door lock. Randy thought he'd ask the Airbnb rep, a college grad with a platinum braid, out after a few screener phone calls. Their interactions on the phone were airy with lots of flirtatious laughter. Meeting in person, their rapport soured quickly. Turns out it was a business braid. It wasn't a fun one like Randy prayed for. I heard their conversation deteriorate through the screen window while I sprayed Clorox on the bathtub caulk.

"And this lawn," the Airbnb representative said right before she left. "You need to mow this. It's probably full of ticks. People notice that kind of thing. They complain when they come home with Lyme disease."

I can tell the last guests were trying to reclaim their youth. I'll be the first to tell you, there's no youth at *The Wreck* to be found. It's just not here. You can read these kinds of guests by the glitter, Burnett's bottles, Dunkaroos wrappers, YouTube history full of '00s Top 40 music and the thrown-up jacuzzi water on the back patio. This is erased with a bag in the recycling can, a full Roku history clear, and a vinegar/Windex/lemon juice solution left to set in the mahogany.

I keep telling Randy to laminate the wood with composite but he doesn't listen. Even Eric, our old landscaper, complained about there being invisible rot everywhere. Eric looked exactly like a stoned version of Robert Redford. Once upon a time he played bass at my church and earned a good living shucking oysters at the Inn kitchens until he stabbed the feeling out of his hand, rendering him unable to do either. Now he lives way down in Sarasota and does nothing but watch the news all day. His former grass grows tall but papery. All of the hardware and sprinkler heads he rigged for his irrigation system are coiled under the deck next to the broken hammock and the cans of beer we used to share after warm afternoons spent landscaping together.

The mess inside is beginning to smell. Boiling a pot of white vinegar and lemon rind will easily cleanse sourness from an indoor setting. The clock on the microwave is fast but I have less than an hour to finish now. For the footprints on the kitchen floor I use vinegar and a quarter bottle of Windex. I saturate my mop and start digging its tentacles into crossing paths of Teva's, bare feet, and tennis sneaker prints. Our girls have since returned to their separate lives again. Maybe forever. It's beautiful in a way, how Randy and I do the Lord's work of staging memories our guests won't know are memories until years from now after they've stopped speaking. I can still hear them laughing over a Spotify playlist, played from someone's phone they put in a mug to amplify the singalong parts. I take the Swiffer from the closet and do a final polish over the last remnants of our girls. I'm sure I hear a car door slam. When I look outside, the driveway is still empty.

The kitchen is the most important part of an Airbnb and the final space that must be returned to the perfection of online photos. Nachos were made here. Sloppy, excessive nachos. Judging by the cheese leading from the counter to the microwave to the linoleum, I can tell their creation was a late-night idea. I'm glad our girls used the can of olives that had been in the pantry since last March because I hate throwing food away. My Swiffer pad breaks apart against the cheese. When I kneel to scrape it off the floor, I catch something flare gold and then white next to the recycling bin overflowing with Truly cans. A heart-shaped locket on a bracelet. Holding it in my hand I can tell instantly how cheap the quality is. Its aluminum hinge has been let in at some dreary department store for someone with particularly small wrists. It goes in the lost and found bag.

The most expensive thing I ever found was a three-stone engagement ring. I remember when I found it I had a horrible chest cold. The ring reminded me of a tiny silver spider with jewels for eyes. I'm not sure if it ever made its way back to the owner. Maybe it was left behind purposely. Once I found a Ziploc bag full of ten-dollar bills and cell phone minute cards that, according to Randy, had to do with drugs. Randy's past as a pill salesman makes him adept at spotting people like that and rejecting their itinerary requests.

To last in the fleeting sanctuary of a beach community, one must hold several jobs. We're a family in that way, the collective staff of every hotel, restaurant, ice cream parlor and kayak rental shop. Our shared goal is to keep visitors at ease. Free from their worries back home. We try so hard to make them forget about where they came from, so I don't fault the evil in those who float over the bridges late at night like reapers on their motorbikes to spread hydrocodone. They're only trying to take how it feels to be on this peninsula and draw it out a little longer. I'm not one for vacations, myself. Life is supposed to be hard. My mother used to say we were like sea glass that way. The smoothest pieces get picked up and collected in small bowls to be left out for everyone else to enjoy.

Two hurricane surges in the last five years have left mold engraved into the popcorn ceilings, and disguised in with the dark of the basement. I think there is no way *The Wreck* can survive another storm. There isn't an insurance inspector in all of Massachusetts with a dumb enough nose.

Last summer when the platinum braided Airbnb consultant left without giving Randy her personal phone number, I had to clean up the mess, but this was more like an overall sort of mess. First I had to console Randy as he watched the consultant's Jetta glide away, crushing crushed conch and scallop shells down the narrow road. I cleaned his emotions up by saying she was a six out of ten at best, and his membership at Planet Fitness was paying off because his biceps were looking so much more defined. Afterward, I had to start our listing over by rearranging the furniture, buying duvets, repainting the sign with a different title, and taking new photos with an expensive camera. We relisted it as the Summer Shack: *Easy living MINUTES from the beach, 10 minutes to the heart of downtown.*

If you're quiet enough through the paperwork process, taking out an extra insurance policy upon restarting an Airbnb listing can be done without anyone noticing. If you can cash it out in time, the representatives usually take a few years to catch on. Whenever they did we would simply start again and rebuild new reviews. Too many hosts do this for the website to ever be able to manage.

Shells crunch from the driveway. I check outside but it's just a car turning around. More diverted beach traffic. Before noon every day, the beach parking lot fills up, and all these people will use the empty half of our shared driveway to get back on Route 17. Randy spent a lot of money expanding the driveway, complaining all the while how the Heffernans didn't offer a dime to help. But I can't remember the last time I saw the Heffernans. All I know is they're boring WASPy folks half retired in a different vacation home somewhere warm year-round. Maybe they live in Florida, like Eric. The Heffernan grandkids were once flabby children covered in ice cream until they returned with skeletal forms that would ease from luxury cars into the daylight where silvery sheens followed their skin to country club tennis courts.

A combination of Drano and boric acid works to unclog the smaller octopus/Provincetown themed bathroom off the downstairs bedroom. One twin bed has been slept in while the other is still made just how I left it a few days ago, with the sheets tucked under the sailboat-patterned quilt. The room is sour from the perfume of the girl who last slept here. Her phone charger is still hanging out of an outlet.

In the living room, I straighten the couch's cushions and non-slip mat beneath the nautilus-print area rug. The copy of John Grisham's *Camino Winds* we use to buffer the couch's craggy spring, is still in place. I find it interesting that the books we keep on the shelves are never examined. There could be all kinds of nasty things written in them and neither Randy nor I would ever know. From the crooked area rugs embedded by crushed

Dunkaroos, I can tell our prior guests tried to rediscover their youth through dancing.

I was twenty-six a few times. One balmy August night at the hotel bar next to St. Jonathan's, I fell in love with a college kid from Cotuit who was there to study horseshoe crab blood for his summer apprenticeship. He brought me to Veterans Park beach (they all do) to show me how these crabs shed their rind at dusk. We swam drunk out to where the millionaires parked their sailing yachts in the cove. This was before I knew about the wreck. Before reality grew so untrustworthy. This young biologist and I were able to clamber up one of the parked forty-footers where we spent the night, living off a stash of ranch dressing and probably very expensive, very ancient champagne. A trillion apricot flavored bubbles passed back and forth in the glass until only spit remained. The kid woke up before me and swam back in the dark but I didn't care at all. I just stayed there on the boat like it was mine. I opened every cabinet, and before swimming back I turned our ranch dressing packets inside out to create metallic shells and left them arranged side by side in an ashtray.

The real wreck was born from two ships destroying each other in the cove. During World War II, the cove was America's eastern seaboard defense. Fort Hill sailors hunted for enemy vessels through their turrets or out on patrol boats. It was a fall morning in the trickling days of the war when PT-280 felt daylight on its hull for a final time. Maybe leaves were rolling on the calm surf. Maybe the Americans displayed a jack-o'-lantern on the bow. German submarine U-67 crawled below, daring closer after having followed the PT boat up coastal waters, waiting until the right moment to rise from its lurk and fire upon the Americans with cigar torpedoes. The Americans knew the submarine was trailing them. They tried steering the Germans toward a trap where gunners were positioned at the fort. PT-280 never made it. The first torpedo skimmed its hull and drifted off like a wayward meteor. In immediate retaliation, the Americans released depth charges everywhere the Atlantic surrounded them with its darkness. *Give 'em their ass's back!* They hollered as if it caught in a bar fight. A second torpedo penetrated the submerging net of propane tanks and struck PT-280 dead on. Depth charges bloomed against the submarine and they both capsized like two animals in a fight to the death, drowning in one another's arms. The short-lived blasts went quiet, leaving an oil slick spreading out as a rainbow.

No guests who stay at the Airbnb know about what the wreck attracted, because anyone who lives around here year-round doesn't talk about it. What's down there hardly ever comes up as far as I know. At night you can hear the things chirping to one another. Eric used to say when we had porch beers that it wasn't them chirping per se, it was how the crickets bent their voices to warn us about them, and I'd say *Eric, you're just too much*. This would be after I helped him bury his tree seeds in the landscape. Now I look at what we planted and it's all grown so out of control. I think maybe he would've liked that.

Time and ocean water turned the once separate sea vessels into one snowy sculpture. Given the chance, I'd renew the wreck in a heartbeat. I think of this often. Of gliding down to it and shaving the coral off the sailor's skulls where Bazooka Joe rests still in their jaws. Bleaching the crushed Honduran mahogany. Scrubbing the iron rails clean. Sweeping the debris into a rubber toothed dustbin. The things down there would put me on their NO-KILL list and after I was finished and safely back on shore, they'd find a bowl of pine cones.

If you want to hear them, those things in the wreck, they usually get busy between ten and midnight, from May to late August. If you know what to listen for, their calls resemble a washing machine full of wet dimes. A long time ago, the town tried drowning them out with nightly drive-in movies.

Randy has no idea how good I actually am at painting. I used to paint portraits of sundaes for ice cream parlors. Now I know how to fix burst pipes and cast mold away with just a little chlorine. The lettering on the new sign, especially the C's, are way better than what Randy tried originally. C's are like whipped cream ripples. Hot fudge is one long W.

The dryer's belch announces that the bed sheets and towels are finished turning. When guests are here we keep the basement locked. I've heard this cottage is the only one on the street that even has a basement. Most people with cottages have to keep their out-of-sight things where anyone can see them. As I scrape lint from the trap I hear a car door and almost roll my ankle jogging up the basement stairs, but it's only someone outside dumping their cooler in the driveway. Sandwich baggies stick to the tires of another car turning around. My brain feels like I've left it drifting in whatever room I've just been in. It could be the fumes. I open two windows to cross-circulate the air.

Once, crumpled up next to the upstairs master bedroom garbage can I found a list. It was written on torn yellow notebook paper and titled *here are 8 ways the beach is trying to drown you*. Seeing this note got me very nervous, thinking someone was on to us. On the entry's bottom it read in summary: *the only place I feel safe is in this beach house, even though I know people have brought their dogs here. it is readily apparent now that true human fear is evoked by unsettled cottages and beach houses because those fears were entangled in our very instincts before cottages and beach houses ever came into existence. like the longest armed anemone, the beach employs lures to catch its prey. it keeps its kill forever, collecting death. depositing death in many rooms. in each seashell there is the humidity of what once lived there. it can be deduced, conclusively, that the beach is simply one big outdoor haunted house. not the real kind. the kind you pay to visit with your friends.* When I double-checked the itinerary to find who wrote the list I assumed it would be drug-addled kids who slipped through Randy's screens, but when I saw it was a distinguished physics professor from Harvard with a website listing public speaking appearances, the hair stood up on my arms and I tore the list into shreds. I took the shreds to the tree Eric and I hand-scooped a pocket of dirt for and buried the puzzle in its shadow.

Where our beers once made fossils in the dirt have since faded along with Eric and I's almost thing. I used to pour over Eric's mindful, bear-like hands and how he didn't throw up too much when he drank. Randy even assumed we had been secretly boning, and there was one evening where it could've happened. We had shared a twenty-four rack at the beach to celebrate Labor Day. We read bible verses, sang Christmas songs and smoked his weed. I kept thinking he'd lean in, but it never happened. I kept thinking maybe I'd lean in, but I never did. There was just something overly superstitious about him.

"You gotta get out of here before it's too late," Eric said, sitting beside me at night in the sand where people usually say things you'll remember forever, because at night in the sand it's just their voice floating in your brain. He said, "That creek is changing in a not-so-great kind of way. Haven't you noticed the oil slicks on the surface? The sulfur smell? That's them. I think they might be evolving. Coming out from where they started, you know?"

He was right about the sulfur. For as long as I can remember, there had been a breakfast sandwich fart hanging in the hotter afternoons. Before our tourism council cut the marine biology grants, the students said it wasn't the marsh dying but something else, and they were real close to figuring it out. In their findings were diagrams that showed strange gradients marking deviations in the water density above the wreck. Grants were revoked and students were forced to turn in all their research. All the floppy discs and notebooks were put in laundry bags and thrown in the cove.

The last real beach day I had was with my sister, Tash, when she was visiting with all four or five of her kids from Arizona. She refused to eat any seafood, saying her husband told her that our shellfish was imported from Maryland. We got drunk off mango IPAs and I told her more than I should have about the wreck. Terrified, she told me I needed to leave before blacking out and forgetting it all. I thought maybe that was good she forgot, because I'm pretty sure it's super against the rules to tell even your only sister from Arizona about what's down there.

The next afternoon at the beach, Tash wouldn't stop talking about how unusual the sand was. *It's too crispy!* She said. She refused to let her youngest son swim. For a moment then I thought that she secretly remembered everything I told her and had gained omens from her drunk dreams. In reality, she was only channeling her chemist ex-husband. Both Tash and I had a thing for scientist types. We speculated this came from our upbringing in the Silver Springs Christian Fellowship Family. That maybe we rebelled by only boning men with logical, scientific minds.

In her broken camping chair, surrounded by beer cans, Tash said, "This nice public beach you've so graciously parked us at? This is nature's basement. And bath-like surface temperatures with low salt levels are perfect conditions for phytoplankton to form." This was her ex-husband speaking. Her ex-husband who dated his students. Who she still longed for and was pretending was here by pretending to be him.

"At least we're together," I said.

"You can see it from here. That muddled raspberry. It's disgusting."

"I don't see anything," I said.

"Ingesting even a sip of it will affect your cognition forever," she said, polishing off her beer and opening two more. One of her kids carefully smoothed the sand around where they had upturned a bucket. I could tell he was on the hunt for a shell with which to christen his tower.

"Look at those teenagers out there. Splashing each other like nothing else matters in the whole entire world except how much sun there is at this moment. They won't remember. Phytoplankton goes right for the mind," she said.

"Oh, that's not so bad," I said.

"Oh, that's not so bad. Of course. Not so bad. The algae probably only eats the inconsequential parts of your memory like the tenor of your grandmother's voice, right?"

"Our grandmother's voice," I said.

"We'd be so lucky," she said.

"Bob would've like it here," I said to push her buttons.

"He didn't have time for places like this," she said to push mine.

A few months later, we stopped speaking after a drunk fight in the comment section of a horse photo our aunt posted on Facebook. For that mess I left out a bowl of sand dollars and blue jellybeans.

If you can go long enough without talking about a certain something, or writing it down, that something can eventually die forever. All the different people who sleep in *The Wreck* are safe in this ignorance. They are without any idea of what's down just past their perfect view of where the tidal grass chops up the marsh.

Thank the Lord. Randy calls me and says our guests got stuck in traffic so they're not going to be here until three. I lie, saying I'm just about finished cleaning out the fire pit in the yard. Randy's reception is poor due to its coming from the Berkshires, the polar west of Massachusetts, where he's gone to meet a woman he's been chatting with on Christian Mingle. I think maybe he'll find a new, better vacation market in those hills and I can move there too. I could pull Eric's trees out and bring them with us. Maybe I could even uplift the grass and transport it in squares to our new homestead.

Realizing suddenly I've mixed vinegar with something blue, I dilute the solution on the kitchen floor by splashing an entire bucket of water on it. Never mix vinegar with anything blue. How could I forget this? I open every single window and take a fan from the upstairs closet. Hair ties are thrown away whole. Cheez-Its. Beer bottles with limes trapped in them forever. By the time I leave, I'll have completely reset *The Wreck/Summer Shack* back to her original state.

You're a shitty ship in a bottle, you're a shitty ship in a bottle, I sing, placing the last of the recycling on top of the seltzer cans. I tie up the bag and leave it on the front deck. Shells crunch under tires. A car door slams. Another opens and chimes over two voices. Randy fucked up. The guests have arrived early. I need to think of a distracting thing to say. A distracting way to greet them because they're about to live out the *Summer Shack's* worst review, but when I look out the window I can tell immediately they're not yoga ladies and they've parked in the Heffernan's side of the driveway. Leaving the car is an older man and woman, both carrying shopping bags and iced coffees. They've brought a possum or maybe it's a dog that's sniffing at the hydrangeas Eric planted for privacy.

"Sir, ma'am, you cannot park in the driveway," I yell out to them from the deck, trying to stay under the roof's shade so they don't see my oversized kitchen gloves.

"We live here," the man says angrily. His chest pokes out like two meaty triangles from a thin golf shirt. His wife is squinting up at me, dressed all in coral.

"I apologize," I shout. "It's just I haven't seen neighbors here for so long. I kind of thought that house, your house I mean, was empty."

"You know, your little internet hotel isn't welcome here. It should be illegal," he says. The woman in coral appears as though she's trying to calm him down, ushering him inside. Three mopeds go to turn in their driveway but the riders have to stop and kick off with their feet, infuriating the man further.

"I only clean the unit," I say. "I clean a lot of them around here, all the way up to Truro."

This causes him to hesitate and then all the anger in his expression leaves so that his face becomes smooth like an overused stair banister.

His wife positions a grocery bag against her hip. "It's not really made from part of an old shipwreck is it?" She asks, and for a second I think she's asking about her husband's face before I realize they haven't seen the newly painted sign.

"Of course not," I say. "It's from a barn. A barn wreck." We laugh.

"Oh, well, that's something. You must find all kinds of left behind things," the woman says.

The man loosens his posture. "Yeah, you certainly must! Say, we've thought about renting this place out and I don't know, you wouldn't mind taking a look right? Like to make a professional assessment?"

"Well, that's not really my job," I say this but I am already drinking palomoas made with Fresca on their back porch. The woman is a very nice former bank manager named Cheryl. Her oversized jewelry clacks against the gnarled bones that jut out from her neck. Their porch is in very poor condition. Milk bottles that appear to have been meant to store beads have been overtaken by rainwater, mildew and dead insects. The couple has a poorer view of the marsh but a better view of the creek. It's a shame they don't use their house more.

Though we don't see it from the back, I can hear an SUV covered in mountain bikes turn around in their driveway. I know it's still got its snow tires by how the shells crunch.

"Goddamnit. Goddamnit," the husband says.

"You're getting worked up," Cheryl says.

"It's the humidity. Lord, is it relentless," I say.

The husband turns to his wife while looking at me. "This is why we always summer on Hilton Head. We just keep this house for the kids. But they barely even use it. I mean, how many months out of the year is this place empty?"

"I like that tattoo on your wrist. What is it?" Cheryl tries to change the subject. She reaches for my arm and holds it in her hand. Her nails look like they were at least four hundred dollars. No brush marks at all.

"I adore tattoos! One of the grands just got one of a bouquet. Her birth flower," the husband says.

"Does yours mean something?"

"Kind of. Have you ever seen the show *Pokémon*?" I ask. A heron distracts us. We all go silent, watching it inch into the creek. Its grace is undermined by the blue feathers it wears like a comb-over. We watch it for a few minutes but it doesn't do anything else.

"Tell us, tell us all about the kinds of things you find," the husband says.

"Well." I sip my paloma, catching a chunk of ice that I swallow whole. "People leave Bibles a lot."

"No, I'm sure they do. The weird stuff. The blood and guts," he says.

"Well, there's not as much left behind as you would think. Nothing dreadful like you're thinking. People have good memories with us," I say.

The wreck is located in a gelatinous aquatic microclimate that proves difficult for swimming. Divers who try making it down there sometimes don't ever make it back up. I think of how it would be impossible to clean them. Once the ocean sinks its claws in you, it can be especially cruel to human forms.

"Oh, come on now, you're holding back." The husband swirls the afternoon into his tequila. Between his stature, his tiny pink head, and the sweater he's wrapped around his shoulders, he reminds me of a periwinkle. Retracing what I've discovered, I try not to squirm in their patio furniture. My mind goes to the bloody peanut butter and jelly sandwich, a sketch outlining the idea for a voodoo doll of Al Gore, a wig stitched to a basketball, and so many handwritten poems. Countless gemstones trapped in cheap mounts, left in ice cubes. A famous actor from California stayed at *The Wreck* while filming a mystery themed cable series that was kind of like the movie *Clue*, except it was rich people thrill-killing each other while placing bets on the police who tried to solve their pre-plotted crimes. I didn't see the ending because it was just too scary. The actor left behind a face cream made from Beluga whale foreskins that made my face look three times younger. He also left behind a sketch resembling a duck with a poem next to it. Maybe it was meant for me, who knows, but I don't mention this to anyone ever.

"You must make a killing renting it out. What do you pull in, five, six thou a month? No, don't tell me," the husband says. He brings up the calculator on his phone, which is trapped in an enormous purple case.

"You'd think so, but the last couple seasons have been rough. With the weather," I say. A voice in my head reminds me not to say anything about the insurance scam. It's not Randy's or my own voice.

The husband clears his throat. Sets his paloma down where it attracts the attention of a mosquito. "She has this idea. It's this crazy thing." He looks to his wife who then begins measuring my reaction.

"You're going to think I'm just full of it," Cheryl says.

"I don't think I understand," I say, but I do. I realize then why they are so friendly. The jewelry outline in their suntans. The diving necklines. The mint on their smirks. The lotion. These are all dead giveaways. They are commissioning me for a threesome. It's obvious. Today is probably even the husband's birthday. I mean of course it is. He's turning sixty or even seventy and they've come to their beach house to celebrate and here comes the maid, of course. I bet they got takeout chicken caesar salad from the place with real anchovies in the dressing. He'll keep his sweater wrapped around his shoulders while he's railing me. It's happened before. It's why I avoid tourist restaurants because tourist restaurants have tourist bars that bring people on temporary departure from the routines that keep them meek. Tourist bars create a habitat for people with no inhibitions. *I can have an extra clam fritter. I can drink and drive. I can be a little too forward with this woman who I'll never run into at my local grocery store.*

"Where's your dog? Didn't you have a dog somewhere?" I ask, but they ignore my question. The husband halfheartedly tries to dissuade Cheryl from asking what she's going to ask. I can't say it's not flattering. Especially since the Lord peaks us all at twenty-six. At twenty-six I was sharp and my eyelids didn't fold over like they do now. My voice was raspy in a way that people thought was cute, instead of now where my vocal cords clench and choke the syllables from my speech. My church band used to put me up front where I would shout psalms beside Eric and Todd with his '80s guitar solos and wannabe Bruce Springsteen headband. The boys even gave me a tambourine and let it slide if I danced up on Todd a little. We'd play bars on weeknights. My ass was higher then so pretty much every drunk in a sunburn would try to buy me fried scallop baskets, because if you want to see the ass without the jeans I guess that's what they felt was necessary, seeing as how a fried scallop basket has exactly 783 milligrams of salt which in turn beckons a pitcher full to the froth with Coors and more Coors, until we'd be drunk, getting air from the view outside where they're talking about how moonlight sticks to water. This even though it would be cloudy. This even though they wouldn't be looking anywhere close to the water.

Your whole interpretation of a place is situated around what interior you've settled in. On this porch, the creek smells more like Easter candy than sulfur. The way shells crunch is louder from here as another SUV covered in bikes pulls in and reverses.

"It's busy for so late in the summer," I say, impressed with my ability to generate small talk.

The husband sets his drink down on the napkin and claps his hands. His palms are very white. Like so white I can see through to the tendons. Cheryl isn't taking her eyes off me. I begin to think of an excuse. After all, I did have to finish vacuuming the mats in the Laguna Beach bathroom. But this sort of people, they'd offer money. Maybe enough to live off for the rest of the year. Enough to go visit Eric. It would be a surprise visit! Everything depends on whether the husband plans on doing it while the wife watches, but usually it's the other way around. Maybe I'll be the one wearing the sweater. In no way am I attracted to the husband, as nothing about him exudes someone who applies science in their thought process. He's an artist type. A curator maybe for Broadway sets or galleries. He probably prefers movies with the little words at the bottom of the screen. I could pre-coat the insides of my legs with the nice avocado oil Randy splurged on for the kitchen. That would trick them. It worked for Todd years ago when we used to go watch fireworks from his van and I'd call him Brucey at the top of my lungs.

The husband dumps the rest of his paloma inside him, sets down the ice, and clears his throat so hard it stretches over his turkey neck bone.

"Okay, so this idea," Cheryl says. "You're going to have to really bear with me here."

"Okay. Alright." I shift in my chair. The cushions are musty from being left outside. I'm ready to name my price. It'll be in the thousands. I'll place my hand on Cheryl's knee as I say it. Then I'll go back across the driveway to quickly finish cleaning. I'll use the Lysol spray as deodorant and shave with the razor in the medicine cabinet of *The Wreck*'s Laguna Beach themed bathroom. Mineral concealer will hide the bug bites on my legs. I'll move my Nissan to the street and change into the shrunken sundress I have in the bag of Goodwill donations in my trunk. Finally, I'll come back over, knock on the door and ask for a drink. Four of them. It'll be temporary and a few hours from now I'll have the money forever. For the mess I will use the flushable wet naps in the upstairs bathroom, the Dr. Bronner's soap in the outdoor shower, and five beers from Amanda at the 99 Restaurant bar.

Cheryl chugs her cocktail and says, "You're going to think we're just nuts." The more she speaks the more a Connecticut accent hardens her words. It's kind of becoming on her.

"I've heard all kinds of things," I say, covering my giggle with a dainty hand. Renovating myself into what they want.

"We call it a meat bomb," Cheryl says.

"A meat. A meat bomb?" I immediately pull back the flirty whisper in my voice and reposition my knees so they're no longer pointing at either of them.

"We'd stow it in the cove, early in the morning before the sun rises but after the lobstermen return. Right when everything's totally quiet. We'd float it not too far, not too close, then detonate it with this remote control." Cheryl produces a five-buttoned remote no bigger than her palm. "The guts and blood would emerge for hundreds of miles down below, undetected on the surface." Her eyes flash. "It would be a feeding frenzy. Especially on a busy summer weekend. Can you imagine?"

"But why?"

"They're attracted to it."

"Sharks?" I ask.

"No, no. The things down in the wreck." Hearing a real person acknowledge them for the first time in so long is jarring.

"It would do a real number on traffic," the husband adds. "After all that death. Oh, those vacationers and their heck spawn would stay clear of here and stick to Squamicut. Keep them off The Arm for as long as we're alive, that's for sure." The husband looks satisfied at last.

Cheryl meets me deep in my eyes. "But that's just a crazy idea. I've always had it. It might put you out of a job though, wouldn't it?"

I laugh to make myself seem less nervous. We revert back to pleasantries and the sun gets behind the clouds. I sip my drink wishing I could spit it out. From here, the tree Eric planted looks like it's growing new crabapples. Teenagers with swimsuits sticking out under their clothes cut through the lawn, laughing and swearing loud enough for us to hear. Their feet are wet, indicating the flooded road hasn't fully evaporated. I imagine the college boy from the sailboat, grown up with kids and sagging jowls. A small ranch off a highway with a basement office with shelves filled with notebooks filled with notes on horseshoe crab blood he tried to retain from his memory.

"Oh, I'm just yanking your chain," Cheryl says. "This remote only works for our deck speakers, see?" She points to a plastic looking rock with dents carved in it. The remote control has BOSE written across the bottom.

"And everyone knows that noise about those things in the wreck is just superstition," the husband says. "Nice to have something among all us locals though. Lord knows it keeps things a little more meaningful around here."

"I'm going to have to agree with you on that one," I say. We remain on the porch listening for more cars. For something to complain about. I can feel the mosquitos starting on my foot veins.

"The days are getting away from us, aren't they?" Cheryl says. "This afternoon light is worth its weight in gold." The heron emerges, bringing with it a silverfish from the slush veined artery of the creek.

"It must be past dinner by now." The satisfaction is gone from the husband's face.

I thank them for the drink. Pat off my pants like they're dusty and compliment their hydrangeas. I make a note to myself that I'll have to water them when their side is empty again.

"Oh, I forgot we have some mail that came for you. Mostly catalogs," the husband says. With all the decorative knick-knacks and furniture we get from there, I know Pier 1 subscriptions will follow Randy and I like a hex for the rest of our lives. Even if we do end up starting over in western Massachusetts.

"He's an odd duck, that Randall," Cheryl says, still looking through the mail.

"Randall?"

"The nervous man I always see outside your cottage."

"Oh, Randy. He owns the property," I say.

"Yeah, I'm not so sure about him," Cheryl says. "I always see him sneaking around at night. He gives me the creeps."

"I'm sorry," I say, instead of prying further. "About all the different people staying here. If it helps, the guests arriving today will probably be on the quiet side. They're those spiritual yoga types."

"Oh, they'll be easy to clean up after," Cheryl says.

Heading back across the driveway I realize I've left the stove on as high as it goes.

MYSTIC PIZZA II

There was something awful about how the phone rang. It spoiled the oven's hum and the patience of gathering snow. The squeak of non-slip shoe on non-slip tile. There hadn't been a call in over an hour, which usually meant they could close early. Giuliana and Ray both looked at the cordless with the same look of disgust, sharing the same thought. We could ignore it. But each ring was trailed by another until she answered it out of breath for a reason she was unsure of, already stabbing at what would be on the other end.

"DeNiro's."

"Hi, can I place an order for pick-up?" A woman's voice said. "I'd like a large small clams casino."

Giuliana scribbled 'CC' on the pad. "Is there anything else? Wait, what size was that?"

"Small. Sorry."

"Alright, will there be anything else?"

Silence. Maybe a palm muting the mouthpiece. Whispers in the background.

"No, that'll do it."

"It'll be about twenty minutes." Giuliana considered telling her it would be longer, as to promote safer travel, but her bitterness towards the stranger had taken precedent. Clams casino was a dish hidden way down on the "Entrees" side of the menu, a rundown neighborhood that also included eggplant parmigiana and veal. It was usually widowers who ordered entrees, or was something added to a stack of pizzas to be thrown on the table during large family gatherings. She couldn't remember the last time anyone had ordered clams casino. It wasn't even the real thing – just spaghetti, marinara sauce, Bac'n bits and clam meat from a can. It was served with a lemon wedge inside a Styrofoam container. Giuliana was positive Ray didn't know how to make it.

Ray had an endless supply of charred dish towels sprouting from an endless supply of acid-washed jeans. His forehead gleamed with sweat. The heat of the ovens would get unbearable in the summer, even with their door open and horseflies pouring in. Now they barely had to touch the thermostat. Ray shoveled a medium hamburg and artichoke into the oven with a dish towel wrapped around his fist, then assured her he could make clams casino just fine.

DeNiro's was just up the road from Giuliana's house on Jesuit Street. She needed the money to pay her college back. She told her grandmother before leaving that she was dropping down to part-time for the Spring semester.

"It didn't use to be we had all this panic," her grandma said, pouring generic brand Pringles onto a plate, eating them without looking down while watching a game show unfold and praying out loud for the contestants. "It's New England. It snows here."

"That's prerecorded, Grandma."

"Well, I'll see you in the morning. Don't slam the door when you come home."

Inside DeNiro's were sepia photographs of Old World people holding baskets overflowing with produce. They hung on the walls next to a chalk sign for buffalo wings. Most of the photographs showed a woman whose eyes were contained within leathery pouches. Giuliana figured she was probably long dead. Her boss had bought the vintage photographs at a tag sale, along with a trophy capped by a brass chef he displayed on top of the soda cooler.

"Wait, I don't think we have clams," Ray said.

"They're there." Giuliana stepped out into the snow, pursued by the parlor's balmy innards. She couldn't see the road from the parking lot but could see the roofs of cars gliding past. A few of them fishtailed, almost touching one another. Even the convenience store two fronts down had closed early. "Look at this," she said. "We're totally left behind." Their plow guy was named Barry or Terry or something that sounded like 'dairy.' Giuliana could never remember it. Sometimes he would stop in and get a meatball grinder with American cheese and a soda to use as a mixer.

Ray found the clam meat and opened them to years of pressure escaping under the can opener. Spirits of farm raised mollusks raced to die in the overhead light. Ray had learned to cook at a Cajun themed chain restaurant called Adelaid's. His forearms were hairless and singed by scars that seemed to glow. Giuliana was wary of him because she heard he had titty fucked the newest waitress at DeNiro's. They both shared the same first name, except the other went by Julie. Julie was a germaphobe or religious or afraid of getting pregnant or something. She didn't want to touch Ray's boner, even though she would pick fries out of other people's orders and peel pepperonis off pizzas before they went out. On several occasions Giuliana saw her scooping sour cream from the Tex-Mex calzone with her index finger.

But Ray didn't act interested in Giuliana. She thought maybe she wasn't stacked enough, but then again, she'd make him look bigger. *It's not my fault Julie's birth control makes her boobs huge.* On a slow night, it was the kind of place where people like Ray would test their prowess on people like Giuliana. One thing leading to another right before actually culminating in anything.

Thirty-five minutes passed, and then an hour. Ray was scrolling through Facebook on his phone. They cleaned everything, even taking the time to wipe the grime beneath the counters with the industrial strength stainless steel polisher that made their hands pink. A van approached but didn't stop. Their cars were the last two in the lot, his a Dodge Neon with its windshield wipers pointed at the storm, shot up with rust by the wheel wells, hers gone inside a cocoon.

"This is why you ask for the number," Ray said, without looking up from his phone.

"We'll wait another twenty minutes at the most, then we're locking the door," Giuliana said.

"She's probably driving real slow. She's going to come all this way and we'll be closed. That's not right."

Giuliana rearranged the business cards, thinking of her grandmother shoveling their driveway. Pulling in to see a mound of snow with a big purple mitten sticking out, Bringle crumbs clinging to her chin hair.

"Jesus Christ, what's taking her so long," Ray said. "She's getting a cold casino."

"She'll be here, she'll be here."

Giuliana regarded the lone plastic bag with its handles knotted.

A wind started up and herded the snow into a million different directions. The ovens had finally gone cold and she considered putting her jacket on. Ray was messaging Religious Julie on Facebook now. She could see her profile picture from a mile away. An old prom photo with everyone else cropped out. Slim senior year jawline.

"Wait, are you guys dating?"

"Pretty much."

"But she's, like."

"What?"

Giuliana felt suddenly odd, knowing she and Religious Julie wore the exact same waterproof North Face parka in TNF black. They were also both Sicilian granddaughters who held their 12th birthday at the same Laser Quest. She imagined some hidden personality between the two, some redeeming qualities that weren't immediately apparent. Her boss said Julie made Ray wear a condom, even just for putting it between her boobs.

Their plow guy forced snow across the lot, into big piles under the streetlights, bringing his scoop down reckless and loose. He left the engine on while throwing salt on their sidewalk, as if seed to geese.

"Who cares what that stupid titty-fucker thinks," Giuliana said under her breath while she turned the sodas in the cooler to face out. The one in front said *Share a Coke with Elias*. One day some weirdo named Elias will buy this Coke, she thought. The door chimed to her back. She turned to see it was just Dairy.

"You guys are still here?"

"Still here," Giuliana said.

"It's getting bad. You should think about calling it a night."

"What can I get you? Nice meatball sub?"

"My wife packed me crackers and hummus, so I'm set. But I'll grab a soda."

He paid with a freezing cold five-dollar bill. "Seriously, though, nothing gets easier as time goes on."

"What?"

"I said it's not going to be getting any easier as the night goes on."

When his truck pulled out, Giuliana saw the ash on the sidewalk had turned full-on pink. "He's right, we better get going," she said. But it was then that a PT Cruiser festooned in wood paneling eased up to the sidewalk. Out of it came a woman whose entire outfit was capped by fur, from her earmuffs down to her boots.

"I'm so sorry," she said, rushing up to the counter. Her voice left her gradually and stretched like how it was over the phone. It matched the parentheses around her mouth. She removed a mitten to wipe off the chip on her card. Giuliana became struck with guilt, trading her the bag of clams casino she knew was cold. The woman did not make small talk about the weather, which Giuliana appreciated. She was a new kind of comfort.

"Can I warm it up for you fast?" She asked. Ray was pretending to sweep, brushing an immaculate floor. He turned off a light in the back. The woman did not seem to be put off by this.

"No, no, it's fine. Thank you," she said.

She left, and that was when Giuliana saw the boulder-sized head filling the front seat of her running PT Cruiser. The head had no body but was alive, Giuliana was sure of that. As the woman opened her door, the dome light showed veins coursing its hairless peach skin. Giuliana heard Ray shuffle from somewhere in the back. The head looked tired but without any real worry, and did not react to the woman getting in and reaching to place the bag down. It simply stared ahead through the grazing of windshield wipers. Her car glided forward, jostling him into the seatbelt as if he were a buoyant child. Giuliana watched the brake lights and turn signal until the car was gone in the storm.

"Did you see that?"

Ray returned wearing his jacket. Pizza box tucked under one arm with the other floating by Giuliana's waist. They were standing in almost total darkness.

"I'm going to go," he said. "It's going to take me forty-five minutes to get to Julie's."

"I just saw something."

"What?"

"I don't know, it was-" Ray watched her impatiently. "I don't know what it was."

"Seen that before."

Before locking the door Giuliana flicked off the By the Slice's neon cursive with the Miller Light sign.

"You need help cleaning off your car?" Ray said, solvent escaping off the both of them.

"No, no, I'll see you. Be safe."

In the great belt of the parking lot, Giuliana audited the tire tracks as if they were prints belonging to an animal. They would be erased eventually, or stiffen into a fossil by morning. From the plaza, the traffic crawling over the highway sounded like a prerecorded version of the beach. She found her ice scraper in the backseat and set to work.

SEAFOAM GREEN

I leave the Sarah Palin mask on his face. The second date is the one that's extra weird. I'm not sure if she is serious about robbing the Edward Jones office. I tell her that financial advisors don't keep actual money. We order gelato, which is ice cream made with eggs. Waves form a blanket to suck tidal pools out from the coast and tumble its sand before crashing down on the plate of an entire continent. You tell me you're also an artist but I can already tell by the loose fit of your biker gang vest. Seagulls are crows at night, are vultures to clean up the body. The withdrawing tide paints this beach with a new shade of green every time. Pitch pines will take over the landscape after a fire. It's soil with a higher sand to dirt ratio they prefer, which is why they're everywhere around here. It's why the Christmas Tree Shops were invented here. And that's what I do, I tap them for syrup. It's not as good as maple syrup, because of the bitterness, but if it's the holidays I'll add Sweet'N Low. I scraped the bottom of my gelato cup until I hit land. I left picnicware in the body. I let walls I've repainted over and over begin to dry out. We found the Halloween masks next to a folding card table at a tag sale, so they were untraceable by the FBI. I hold the handle part of the plastic silverware tighter than I have ever held anything and that includes you know what. To hold the money it's a tote bag lined by vegetable carcasses. The thing about summer is that you can trace the beginning of each one to a specific moment. Usually it's a gradually warming afternoon or when birdsong starts to filter in from outside your window and you think, I should open this window. You told me if that moment happens at night, it's a bad omen, but I'd say that's just a young wive's tale. Our town voted to build a statue of a famous octopus for the town center rotary. The Sarah and I painted eyes on a hundred seashells, using clear nail polish to create a reflection on their surfaces. I swear to God once near that Instagram-famous carousel I saw a gull cleaning a wedding band until it was skull white. The carousel's horses are not based on actual horses. These horses were dreamt up. Goldwater's fist closes on the sap tongue and half sap leaves a smell on the night. The claws of your grandmother's couch leave a pilgrim hat shaped gash on the wall. I'm searching for where The Sarah mask lets him see, where it oozes at the collar but doesn't stain. Closer than he's ever gotten. He raises his arm high above my head and floats it there for a moment. My body cannot digest his clothes. A truck with a Barry Goldwater '64 bumper sticker brought in the pedestal for the octopus monument. It is distinguished for having eaten like three people after swimming up a saltwater creek. The octopus, not the truck. We have beach bodies now. Everyone, and I mean everyone, wears a sweatshirt on top and shorts on the bottom. I return the stereo behind the cash register to *Adult Island Rock 107.9* instead of static. These families turning over my candles for the price sticker are happy at once. Feeling something isn't hard. It's feeling something at the same time as someone else that is. Only at night did the families abandon our peninsula, leaving us to drink from a bucket filled with our collected sweat. The dog barks at the dead lady that used to live in your apartment. We become fast friends. She teaches me how to cheat at cribbage. On the bathroom wall there is a sign that says: *Live. Laugh. It's not the victims of your botched heist that stay, but the stupid politician masks you bought at a tag sale as your disguise that will follow you forever.* I can't read because I'm blinded by shampoo with her seated on the toilet and me taking a shower. The film of teeth bleaching strips goes soft in my stomach. When the shower floods we are like the dead lobster divers we drove over when we crossed the Bourne, singing that one song in the car. It's the warmer months when the beach feels almost dead, not the winter, not like everyone says on TripAdvisor. In the middle of summer, everything that could've happened, all the possibilities you imagined have already come and gone. Winter is when you can dream. We like it like this, when the beach has those 'sooty windows of the Victorian style house that no one fixed up after that fire' vibes. It's gross and it creeps you out because you heard three people died from smoke inhalation, but the possibilities for rebuilding are endless, and therein lies the promise of it. The Sarah's face melted into that of Goldwater's, we think. Everything is sticky. The hum of young families lingers a little on the beach, but it'll go away. Except for the looks that husbands steal from their new wives across double mocha chip while their children sit unaware of everything that came before them — those expressions stay floating in air. I can see the faces sometimes when I go by the stacked up Adirondack chairs by our donut shop. The second I focus, they're gone. We recall our winter bodies. The same ones that we used to meet one another. A candlelit dinner setting doesn't show shell meat sucked out to leave an empty house. The walls of suburbia before Christmas where everyone was making out. Stove smoke made it hard to talk. The walls were being smoothed by wet paint. That winter is still alive somewhere else.

It can always be painted over. Wallpaper or oil based primer over wallpaper. The lady barks at the dead dog that used to live in your apartment. The way she clicks her tongue sounds like the tacky sound a foam roller makes. Portraits glow within undersea caves. Maybe they've been composed with toxic paint. There's a special part of a creek where the freshwater part overtakes the saltwater part and no matter how sinister a sea beast you are, you're going to have to face the music and turn around. I could live in memories of being sick with someone's palm over me. A husband or anyone, I literally don't care who's palm it is. We just want palms. I asked Goldwater, where do tourists go when they die? You told me they go to Tourist Heaven. Do you have a minute to hear about the cleansing properties of gull saliva? Behind the apartment's dishwasher there was an entryway to another dimension. I heard the biker gang who claims the insignia on your vest killed like four people in a hotel bar fight after a corporate team building event. Goldwater was afraid of coming indoors. The Sarah was afraid to come indoors. Driving home at night I'd decorate the empty, off season roads with pepper whiskey. At a strobing gold light, I'd wait for him to cross. The octopus monument is pretty fucked up looking in the dark. They got its face all wrong. Its brow was less furrowed in real life. Teenagers gather by the octopus statue at night. I've heard their prayers. The off-season hookers here swim in sweatshirts and spandex bike shorts. They love 90s thrash metal. Katy C. can create a bong from thin air and she tells me about her sisters in Brighton while we sit on your grandmother's old couch. You fall asleep. I watch The Sarah move from one side of the room to another, casually like it was wetting its rubber mouth with tap water. 'Can't you see it? I'll protect us both if I have to.' But it was useless because The Sarah is a vanishing monument to a heist gone terribly wrong. Nail polish gives only an illusion of newness. A New Yorker tote gives the illusion of not being stuffed with miniature liquor bottles. Then I was overcome with a sunburn. One that slowly paralyzes its victim before sucking out the guts. It does feel better coming outside, we said. Two Gal's Treasures & Knick Knacks will now close at three pm. The other Gal wanted to call it SheSirens. The other Gal destroyed our dream by fatally stabbing an Edward Jones advisor. There's a special part of a summer anthem where the synth part overtakes the static part. The people in our shop bought more saltwater taffy when it came on so we played it over and over and over. When pulling my clothes up over my head, I would panic. I knew Goldwater was there. In the shower when I washed my face and my eyes were clenched shut I knew he was right outside the door. I could sense his shape behind blurred glass and I would have to force open my eyes, stinging from shampoo, to make sure. You said, I think the water is coming from inside the dishwasher. It's only ever twenty dollars to park when everyone wants to be in the same place as you. At the luau themed birthday party we talked about how they found still frozen shrimp in the rubble of the Victorian home that almost burned down. This was when the hula girl pulled us into a bathroom hung with faux-aged boards on which things were written like *May you Always Have Shells in your Pocket & Sand Between your Toes.* Next to other people's toothbrushes, I expected The Sarah to reappear. I held onto her the second hardest I've ever held anything. Hands hooked with our ribs passing and building a bonfire of nervous energy before extinguishing its wild reds with garments soaked to transparency. Disappointment when the faux aged boards turned out to be just for decoration. We sit on the rim of the bathtub, smelling each candle. If these walls could talk! The hula girl says. They can't talk, but they can hear, I say. We pass out in someone's parent's bed. When the comforter recedes there's kelp, carnation blossoms, warming grape flavored jellyfish, horseshoe crabs. Did you know washed up horseshoe crabs are actually just the molted husks they've left behind? You're mourning them in your grey college sweatshirt. In cutoff jean shorts and they're swimming around, laughing at you. Inside where it's lush, where bucking couches roam, the color has completely dried. You can touch it and nothing comes off. It's not fair to the dust that gets trapped under the paint. It's not fair that the lady who used to rent this house has to get trapped beneath whatever color we felt partial toward that day in Lowe's, drunk off 99 Restaurant margaritas. In warmth the husbands return with new wives. His nails have made glowing crescents inside her. Together they linger in mountain laurel exploding from branches that once reached out as scaffolding, now offering folded blooms. In the car we decided who would wear what mask. It was hot enough to melt latex. Dread still rests on old snow. After, I insisted we put the masks on the victim so everything would look like a weird suicide. It was you who insisted we keep the masks on in the hotel bed and then it was Goldwater on top of me who could not hear the singing from the next room. The anthem of a dead summer plodding through wet walls. Drunk prayers hot on my neck, swallowing a mouthful of Gillette and wet paint. Navajo White on Eggshell. They used that on all the developments. Two kids staining the air of new beginnings. On the bathroom wall there is a different sign made to look homemade:

You ask what New England is like. If it's like Christmas all year and how it feels, pretending to be a Kennedy in the summer wearing a little pink whale on your breast. We use our beach bodies as vessels to travel through time now. The first portal didn't hurt one bit! Beneath a comforter I looked down for a second. In all your blackest paintings there were these mountains in the background that I didn't notice at first.

126

PAPER OCEAN, PAPER FOREST, PAPER SUN

1.

Beyond the cracked sidewalk, and the telephone pole with a rainbow of flyers, and the patch of dry grass, there stood a ten-foot-high concrete block wall, caked with coats of paint. At the foot of it was a shrine. Some burnt-out candles, dead flowers and a few soggy teddy bears. One word of graffiti filled the wall: Rejoice!

"We did it, Nan. It's ours again," Barbara said, gesturing behind us at the gift shop windows above the marsh now visible beyond an empty public lot. "It's truly ours." I could tell she was numbing her worry by how she smudged her dolphin pendant. A gift from her husband that reigned over the freckled triangle of her chest, still glowing from the summer.

But summer was over now. Canned up, sealed and labeled with the rest of them at the warehouse. We could comfortably stuff our toes back into jelly sandals for a while and cross the street without worrying about colliding with drunk tourists on their rentals. These accidents happened so often that eels started creating nests in the blanched memorial Vespas that were lost over the bridge. Without tourists, the canal's slime seemed to smell more brackish, or it could've been that I only took notice of this in their absence.

Barbara looked exactly like a woman who would infinitely be a Barbara, with her gingivitis and keyhole turtleneck that was flaccid from the dryer at our shitty Laundromat. Once she was an infant named Barbara and would be one again if reincarnated. I told her we should bail to nab frosé and scallop fritters one last time, but before we could leave we were interrupted by another local who seemed to be on his way to stack timber or manage a quarry. Taking off his gloves and quadrupling his hands, the man got to talking with Barbara. I didn't listen but I watched his chin, which was familiar. It jumped up and down like a perfectly round, speckled stone you'd drop in a stream to smooth its edges. They say the harder the jawline, the more distant the husband. I thought of carving that into a plank of driftwood.

He asked us if we had seen the 'you-know-what' and asked about our favorite parts of summer as if we were kids returning to school. I gave him nothing until he left us alone to rejoin the group now congealing for our main event. They were flooding the base of the wall to get a better view of a fifty-foot-tall papier-mâché man wearing giant cargo shorts with pockets made from fishing nets. He wore crude sandals with Velcro large enough to snare a bird, and socks that stayed stiff in the breeze. Beneath a shirt for a basketball team I heard of once, they had given him a humble chest. The mayor, a Kennedyesque young man who tucked his necktie into his windbreaker, was having difficulty adjusting his bullhorn's volume. Though flanked by chaperones, they offered no help.

'You-know-what' was how we politely indicated there was a bog witch in our midst. The rumor germinated quickly. She smelled like vermouth and could walk without touching the ground. She had traveled across six different dimensions to assume potions from our dreams and to bite us in our sleep. Others were convinced she wasn't actually visible, only a scarecrow sewn from our own excitement and fears. I imagined her with claws made out of fabric.

The scandal was what we needed, now that we were without the drama that visitors brought. Their sad marriages, their photography of us in front of sunsets. Their obsessions with gelato and lobster rolls. With the effigy looking toward the crowd, desperate for someone to help, I felt sad for it. Part of me wanted to cut him free so he could find a papier-mâché wife just a few feet shorter than him and settle down somewhere away from us. Who could blame him for wanting a getaway? Someone threw a glass Frappuccino bottle at him that shattered on the brick, to which someone yelled, no glass allowed!

"The entire shore is glass, really, if you think about it," a lady next to Barbara said. I chose to be perceived as a quiet, mysterious type at the burning. Last year I was a debutante, having my knuckles kissed, laughing and bucking in wild gestures. This year, rather than gabbing with our fellow locals, I stayed inside my own head, licking the sweaters that set across the back of my teeth.

My clothing reeked of bakeries and children due to my living off fudge for three months. I needed new clothes anyway, but the fall Penny's catalog had not arrived in my mailbox yet. The summer issue's direct number had been disconnected. But they're all wondering, I can tell. *Why is Nan so quiet, so mysterious? Look at her. Imagine what secrets she must have, how bored she must be of this place and its rituals.* Part of me was fearful, convinced in the bog witch's plan to start slaughtering us the moment the effigy was lit.

"I miss them, Nan. I know they're awful and bring so much misery, but I miss them." The Barbara had a point. The tourists weren't all bad. Sometimes they'd bring us houseplants wrapped by stories that took place in glass buildings. Stories about cousins who were fingerless from holding M-80s too long. Barbara caressed her dolphin even harder, polishing its rainbow oil surface. It was appraised at well over a thousand dollars on account of the eyes being real diamonds. A month ago she gave me a bracelet for my birthday (which was actually in December), that I never wore because it left green splotches on my wrist.

Every time The Barbara went quiet, I got paranoid she had noticed her missing gift and I'd check to see if she was frowning at my splotches. Just above them was a letter D drawn ornately in ink. I don't remember receiving this because when I got it I was very young or very drunk, which they sometimes say are the same thing. Decades of direct sun blurred the marking as if I had tried to wipe it off and it got stuck that way. There are procedures, I've heard, to have these things scraped off.

A shrieking came from the parking lot. At once we thought it was the bog witch unveiling herself to us with a knife to open our throats but it was only our town trucks removing speed bumps for the plows.

"Look at them. Overpaid dentists digging out an overripe molar," Barb said.

We turned our attention to the snapping noises above us, to the cables hoisting up The Albert's shoulders, and watched Miss Cape Cod 2011 touch the beacon to his gas-soaked clothes. The mayor watched her hungrily. Some of the sparks rained down and briefly ignited the candles. All expensive, hand-dipped wax jars from conch., our town's flagship boutique. The effigy's bald crown became alight with pointed flames. Its paleness turned to charcoal. There was a great rousing gasp which weakened to hissing as the flames receded to reveal a wiry skeleton, forced by heat to wave at us as he died. We all clapped at once. Something brushed my leg and thinking it was the bog witch I let out a word somewhere between help and Barbara. She shot me a look. A cat scampered away from beneath us, its fur like the bristles from an old dish brush.

"Rejoice, rejoice." The mayor led a chant, though I only lip-synched along. "The sightseers are gone from us." They would be remembered as those who imagined they lived here too. Fairweather friends with important jobs who came to drink our chowder, take photos before our mural backdrops and fuck on our beaches. Barbara was the only person I knew who had fucked on the beach, but she was also the only person I knew. She wasn't watching The Albert's torched corpse anymore, but rather something by the docks. She asked me if I recognized him. Him? I followed my friend as she walked away because I didn't want to be left alone. The ashes reminded me of how much I was dreading winter's stagnant iced coffee cauldrons and joint pain that was already beginning to set in.

The jellyfish were said to be volatile this time of year when the cove was the warmest and the air was just beginning to chill. At the source of their stings, they tended to leave a throbbing, almost wet sensation. Our library had a hundred books about the 1989 Jellyfish Massacre, when a spawning nest of Portuguese man o' wars killed three tourists and injured countless others. We remembered through graffiti above urinals and a mural that hung in the Town Hall, depicting bathers fleeing from the waves with their tongues puffed out like pink broccoli. If that wasn't enough to keep people from swimming, our strong currents spelled certain death for anyone dumb enough to wade out into them. This was just common knowledge. But we were safe now. The lifeguards didn't screw around. Posted in towers, chained to floats, their eyes were polished binoculars.

At the end of every summer, our tourism council held a funeral for the season as an annual gift to the people who lived here year-round. The ones who contended with storms in fall and protected the precious views from eroding. We singlehandedly kept the boutiques stocked with local crafts. Without our found-object poaching, the gift shops would be nothing but mass-produced Wine O'clock dish towel traps. Later on, there would be a great hootenanny in the old Smithsonian barn where we'd watch the tourism council's brochures disappear in a bonfire. Former love letters from our community resolved to snow.

Barbara yelled at Heaven like she was addressing her dead husband. Her husband was not really dead or at least I don't think he was. Our phones, however, had been dead since the hurricane in August. Its winds took out some kind of tower. Barbara was extra horned up and praying that Ned from the market would be at the hootenanny. She had plucked her chin for the occasion and wore a cowboy hat she said was from her life back home.

We didn't talk about the jobs we held once or whether we were old or new money. It was rude to do so. Barbara gave me a kidney from her clementine. She told me she felt like a new person and couldn't wait to peel off her old skin. Sometimes she'd apply Elmer's glue to her fingers just so she could do it. Under my tongue, the fruit felt like a bitter sack of nothing. I forced it down whole. We left, both with the same tastes in our mouths.

"Don't forget to feed Boomhauer," she said to the coin-operated telescope, which only stared us down with its gut full of quarters. Whenever she was nervous, Barbara got carried away with stories of her dachshund. "Boomhauer was named after his father and his father's father." In the parking lot, we saw the town trucks had left behind fast food bags. Those jerks, I said. We found the beach sitting where we left it. The metal detectors doted along, obeying their masters isolated in headphones. Sometimes one would crouch down and unearth something, the others racing over like gulls to see what had been found. Barbara mumbled about how it was a waste of good shoes, digging around for stolen treasure. When I looked to her it was apparent she had something much more important she was waiting to tell me.

"Someone has been watching me, Nan. At night." She spoke as if reciting cereal ingredients in very small print. I asked her if it was the bog witch, but she didn't know. She said someone was stealing her things too. Moving them around. Items she swore she left in certain places one moment would be gone the next.

It was the part of the afternoon when one's mind baked itself if worked too hard. Grill juice was in the air, mixing with salt and stirring a million things inside me. I remembered Reese's peanut butter cups instead of Hershey bars. Forgetting a sweater in the car. Shooting myself with bug spray point blank until it foamed in the crease of my leg. The husband cooking me s'mores offered black holes warping above his collar. I felt nervous, biting a marshmallow off a stick that had just been in the woods where our dog vomited up grass. Waking up inside a damp, dew-infested sleeping bag. Driving home early through morning fog, back to Delaware. The long way to avoid the city. A psychologist was coaching a man through a divorce on the radio and then they were gone and from the smoke came a woman urging me toward the market. She acted as if we were good friends. I decided to call her Marigold because she reminded me of a perennial. Her hair wasn't naturally gold but who cared to pass judgment on such a pleasant morning? She was scared and trying to cover it up. That I could tell.

"It's normal, I know, to feel as if you're being followed. You don't think someone's actually after me, do you? I mean, there are a lot of women here who might want me dead," Marigold said. I liked her voice. She explained how she spent the night at a suitor's the night before, and had woken up behind the couch holding scissors. "Don't tell anyone, oh no. I don't want the whole town to think I'm losing it." I promised her I wouldn't. I didn't even know who I would've told.

Marigold needed bread. She put air quotations around bread. I had no idea why she was doing this or what the real bread was. My knee was bickering with my back, and the more I tried hiding my limp the more it stung. The market was in between a Laundromat and a shuttered boutique called boate shuze that only sold things with sand dollars on them.

We were greeted by three different kids in aprons. Shelves were lined with acres of laundry detergent being renewed by a girl who grazed them with a feather duster. I hated the market. The overhead lights stung my eyes and it was always filled with awful doo-wop songs played to bare tile. I tried not to step on the darkest tiles, just in case their reflection was only the partially congealed surface of magma. Magma is the 8th leading cause of death amongst middle aged adults. Not a lot of people know that.

Ned, Marigold quietly pointed out, was on a cash register. Another kid with permed hair was popping tape off a stack of boxes. It was Randy, my son. I gave him a hug but his back felt different. It twitched under my arm. "You're not Randy," I said. He shrugged and said he had one of those faces. A man who wore his shirt tucked so far down his pants that it sucked into his navel, came from out of nowhere to yell at the boy. I told him I wasn't sure where my head was, but the man gave me a warm smile and apologized. Both went off to whisper privately about whatever it is men whisper about in grocery stores. Marigold was already strategically picking items for Ned to ring up. Onion powder, rye bread, pina colada-flavored lubricant, and short ribs, because she knew he loved barbecues and would quite possibly offer to cook dinner on her patio.

"You look nice, Barbara," he said. Barbara! That was her name. Not Marigold. She thanked him and turned her face the way people turn their faces when they're drawn in pastel. He asked her about the cowboy hat and ignored the context of her groceries. "I simply have no idea what to do with this much meat," she responded coyly. She acted like one of those women from the infomercials who die with their dish gloves on.

Ned said he probably wasn't going to the hootenanny because he was tired and maybe sick with mono. He wasn't sure yet but was definitely showing symptoms. This made Barbara or Marigold or whatever her name was want to make out with him even more so, I could tell. The Hungry Shirt man appeared again and handed us gift cards for our trouble. I assured him there was no trouble and I was just tired from the day's festivities. His shirt was almost entirely inside his stomach now.

"You know you shouldn't eat that stuff," Ned told her, pulling blank receipt paper out in a scroll. "That meat, it's all packed with sodium. I want to see you eating salmon, Barbara. You need Omega-3." The blush didn't leave her face until we reached the mums display on the sidewalk. Who knew what salmon was code for.

Outside we drank free coffee. It drew acid up from my stomach that tasted like a rotten Christmas decoration. We walked up the bluff where there were several geezers setting up their easels. This was the best view of our lighthouse. From there, its decaying seaweed skirt was almost impossible to see. Standing far enough away, the lighthouse was a beautiful monument made white by the sun's glare.

"Look at those ancient farts," Barbara whispered loud enough for them to hear. One of them turned and bared his freckled gums at us. Good morning, we said. A man inside a helmet of white hair told us we looked particularly lovely today and asked if we had attended the burning. "They really cooked him this time," he said. Another man held his thumb out, measuring the lighthouse. He painted with a set of drab acrylics from a box burned in with cursive. None of them had the wrinkles that came from years of worry. These were sun wrinkles. These people were old money, we agreed.

"Who would want to paint that decrepit silo anyway," Barbara hissed. I pretended to agree, but unlike most Capers I felt pride for our haunted silo. It gave this place character. In the 1950s it had belonged to a dairy farm before Hurricane Edith washed everything away except for the main structure, a rocket frozen mid-flight, shooting out of a peninsula that could only be crossed if one successfully conquered the mathematics of tides and moons. Otherwise, you'd end up like those cows that were delivered right to the bull sharks. There's a painting in the Saint Street Gallery of them, stupefied Oreos toppling in frothy green crests, their faces totally serene as if the waves were just another pasture. The farm was owned by Captain Jan Frances, who wasn't a real captain, but insisted he be addressed as such. After Hurricane Edith made him a widower, the town felt sorry enough to keep the false captain moniker in his name, even etching it to his headstone when he succumbed to bacteria in bad milk. This was not how he actually met his end, but rather a rumor invented to soften the truth.

Everyone knew the story: Captain Jan Frances woke up in the morning beneath perfectly rare ham flesh pulled across the sky. He sat down to breakfast with his wife, Sara, and three children. The redder the sky the angrier the gale, she said, pouring his coffee. He fed the chickens and opened the secondary gate so his livestock could escape in case there was light flooding. He said goodbye to Sara's honeybees because she insisted their yield was sweeter if they were socialized with. Made sure the stove was stocked and exchanged a Folgers-breathed kiss with his wife before leaving to wait out what was predicted to be a mild storm in New Bernard's Tavern, now a boutique called Sailur on 720. According to legend, while the storm battered the tavern, Captain Frances washed down a lobster and a half with thirteen beers and a pound of butter. This was done in the exact future spot of an expired fire extinguisher fixed to a load-bearing beam. The Captain spent the day there mulling about feed prices where tourists would finger Square readers. He threw darts into walls that would someday be hung with watercolors of sandpipers. Outside, the storm had strengthened. Word got to the tavern that the surge had been worse than expected. The Captain rushed home but when he arrived he only found the sea and his silo protruding from it. The storm left no stone unturned. Its fingernails had left large gashes on the cement pillars of the docks. Its vomit riled the bay and turned it to acid.

There was a painting of this in our public library. It did not show the part where Captain Frances took out his pistol that he normally reserved for trespassers and rabid marlin and shot himself in the mouth. It did not indicate that Captain Frances had a predisposition for depression and was possibly allergic to shellfish, which would have put him in a poor, possibly fevered headspace. It did not show his teeth in the soup of smoke and skull. The tavern, the silo, his wife's washed-out beehives, and even that fire extinguisher were drenched in curses. Years of marsh climate eroded what had once been the tower's luminous exterior. You did not go near it and you especially didn't go past to the forest beyond. Everyone knows a forest bordering a cursed landmark acts as the grease trap for its maker's evil. Everyone knows a bog witch can survive in the wild without food or water for up to sixteen years.

The painting, "Lighthouse of the Afternoon," depicted this place with oil on canvas. Our Sunday farmers market sold a Sara Frances brand honey jam. Around the holidays it was available from The Crown & Anchor, an adorable shop right across the street from Sailur on 720. Out of respect to the drowned cows, none of our restaurants served red meat. College kids did the *thirteen beer, one and a half lobster challenge* as a rite of passage. You could get it for $50 with a student ID at the Beachcomber. If you wanted the full glory, you'd finish the lobster's husk with it, antenna and all, just like Captain Frances on that red sky morning.

Barbara and I did each other's makeup outside the hootenanny, where the face of the barn was waking up from its slumber as indicated by lanterns in the topmost windows. A pallet loaded with brochures still in their boxes sat beside turpentine-soaked kindling. Some men in heavy coats were making small talk around a meat smoker that burnt the air and made everything taste like winter. The 80s wedding playlist that thrummed out was waking us up. It was inspiration for the purple rouge I used to recreate Barbara's jawline.

"We're getting fucked tonight, Nan," she said. "Especially you. You need it. You've lost your luster. I hope you don't mind me saying it." Her brush was cold and wet against my eyelids.

At the door, we were greeted by chaperones in pink zebra print cowboy hats. There was rum pineapple mint punch served in a bowl alongside a grinder longer than any sandwich I knew could have been born into the world. The thought of its creator unsettled me. The fact that it was tuna fish put a tight feeling in my throat.

Hay bales had been moved in, but Barbara said not to sit on them because they were infested with pregnant ticks. Chaperones were dragging in a tiki statue that I was almost positive Lee Howardson created. Lee was famous for carving bears out of logs. I wouldn't be surprised if they commissioned him for the tiki as well. His signature chainsaw marks were apparent even from where we stood. I could see how his former lifestyle as a longshoreman had made his incisions sloppy.

"We sprayed them good," Ned said, swiping a hook into one of the hay bales. He had been hired for catering but couldn't stay. He told us they also hired him to clean the bales because last year several people were bitten by straw mites. Mites, not ticks. "Where's your hat, Nan?" I felt him force one down on my head.

When we weren't standing in line outside, we were standing in line inside, waiting to plop the pulled goose meat onto paper plates. There was also cornbread made with jalapenos and something that was either cold macaroni and cheese or warm macaroni salad. Brian, who Barbara slept with sometimes, was there. He had his own Swiss Army steak knife which he used to cut chunks away from the goose and eat with his fingers. They reminisced about how he loved chauffeuring her around in his Camaro, but when Barbara would pick him up in her minivan he refused to sit in the front, choosing instead to hide in the backseat.

"I can't be caught dead in a Ford, let alone a dang minivan," Brian said, laughing out pieces of fowl. I took off the hat and left it in a garbage bag, concealing it beneath my remaining macaroni.

After we finished dinner, two-step country was forced from the speakers. The lap steel made a sound like sizzling wires under the singer's robotic commands. As we stomped, dust rained up from the floor and settled as a sneeze in my face. Our budget must have gotten bigger. Last year they just hooked up an iHome to an old keyboard amplifier. Ceiling rigged lights scanned those brave enough to dance. They kicked the air and thrust their belt buckles at one another. When the song ended a new one with banjo in it made everybody erupt in applause. Even me. The rum made us go off time, so the clapping was more like distant firecrackers. Someone flipped on a fog machine. Spider leg lasers turned pink against the flannel and tight-fitting denim of the frontline dancers. The lights dimmed and darkness placed us all in obscurity, though the chaperones remained with their arms folded in the sawdust smoke, cupping their hands over each other's ears. They'd only stop to mock someone who was extra drunk. Pointing and snickering. What secrets do the chaperones have? How interesting could their lives really be? The tiki statues were the ultimate judge, glowering at us, their bear eyes fiery.

Mrs. DiStefano, who had lived in town longer than anyone, stood alone with her back directly to the largest speaker, clapping along. Every wrinkle on her face was sucked into her grin. That dumb old broad, I thought. But when I saw the chaperones pointing at her and laughing I felt awful and began making my way toward her, dodging the eye contact of cowboys whirling their invisible lassos at me. As the music roared I gently pressed down on her shoulders to guide her away from the speaker's shaking grill. Mrs. DiStefano was a wispy thing and the ease with which she responded felt as if I could've steered her anywhere. Her drooping earlobes, pulled that much farther down by her earrings, were the dice on our dashboard. When we were far enough from the music that I could park her, she asked if I'd seen her father. I figured her father must've been well over a hundred. She said the engine wasn't a quitter. Her father built it, and things DiStefanos built didn't quit. I gave her a ladleful from the punch bowl, which had been moved to look like the tikis were urinating into it, and bid her goodnight.

Barbara found me drinking alone. We went out to the beach where Brian was half stumbling, half shaping driftwood into a tent shape. It was still breezy. Someone's cowgirl hat had blown into where our own bonfire would be ignited. The town sanctioned fire was too easy to skip.

"Capers all taste the same," Brian said with his arms around Barbara. He was being inappropriate. Tomorrow he would apologize and say he had gone too hard on the Captain & Pepsi. Brian was not Barbara's first choice but he would do. Thick wrists, intently shaped sideburns, scarring somewhere on his lip. Boyish face complete with some faint freckles on their way into becoming liver spots. Smelled like toothpaste. Totally her type, even though he was pushing eighty and Barbara was reinventing herself as somewhat of a cougar.

I didn't have the heart to tell her that the younger ones were not interested like how they were in the programs we watched. Ned was just one in a long line of twentysomethings who were unfazed by Barbara's orange flesh and surgically enhanced bust. This didn't stop Barbara from insisting her makeup be mirrored against those women in the decade-old reruns that we'd rely on to get us through winter.

A woman joined us to brag about incorporating sea glass into brooches. She went on about how to effectively stitch an anchor onto a tote bag. Brian said it was best to start from the head, while another person I couldn't make out in the dark assured us it was best to begin threading at the crown. Her teeth and glasses were the only things I could see. After squirting turpentine on the smoldering teepee we were all made orange. Barbara told me she would fix me up with Brian's drinking buddy Joel, who had arrived with a fishing cooler full of beer. When he offered me one I declined, but he had foreseen this and came prepared with frosé.

It felt unsafe to be so close to the silo without being able to see it. This proximity was usually manageable in the daylight, maybe even comforting, because we knew it was a nocturnal creature. Yet there was a sense that it could move around in the dark to appear right beside you. A dog barking off in the distance might be a warning. The bog witch could be lurking just beyond a dune or sleeping standing up in one of the tool sheds. I feared that speaking too loud would attract what lurked outside the safety of our halo.

"Don't look so happy to be here," Joel the drinking buddy said. "You're too cute to worry about cursed barn-jarms." This made Barbara scratch Brian's forearm in jealousy. A subconscious marking of territory. Joel announced that he needed to bleed a lizard before disappearing. I secretly hoped the dark deal made between bog witch and silo would result in him being the first and only sacrifice.

"You'd think with how much I'm paying in taxes we could live in maybe a little less, I don't know, fear," I said, forcing my mouth into a crescent shape. This put everyone at ease. Taxes comforted them. Those reliable obligations comforted me too. The frosé was getting the better of me, which the heat off the fire turned into nothing but warm raisin flavored Gatorade. We clutched our Solo cups as if we were teenagers. If I blurred my eyes enough I'd swear we all were teenagers, maybe circling in a field, a forest, or the yard behind somebody's mother's house.

Brian kicked driftwood in and the fire licked the tip of his boot, causing it to smoke a little. He shrugged back and quietly kissed his cup. "Oh, I miss this," Barbara said. The men made howling noises, pretending to be the bog witch. They slurred ghost stories, now full-blown drunk off tiki urine. I didn't like ghost stories after dark. They made shapes out of the night. Joel came back alive, with an armful of timber. "It's from one of the old lifeguard towers. Pressure treated, I think, but it'll burn."

"You didn't wash your hands," I said. Smoke forged us in purples and greens that could only be conjured by arsenic. Joel gave up and went home with his cooler, taking with him a pond scum smell I was unable to place. Those who remained found solace in embers. The support of the last intact log cracked, finally bringing the teepee down on the half-burned-up cowgirl hat to destroy it once and for all. It smoldered from within like a geode. Then our cups turned into dripping red wax.

The smoke burned my throat and everywhere I tried to move away, it chased me until it became a sort of game. This must've caught the attention of the chaperones because two of them came rushing over armed with Super Soakers. One grumbled that he knew letting us burn anything was a bad idea, and then fired directly at its core. "We're giving them too much freedom," he snapped. From a third chaperone's hands manifested a bucket, and from the bucket came a great pillow of steam.

2.

In the morning, we sat on Barbara's porch and complained about Brian, while breakfasting on Entenmann's and Snapple tea warmed up in her best faux bone china. We watched the gulls bounce among washed up crabs, daring closer to the metal detectors before being startled off by chirping whenever one found a fishhook or coin. In an attempt to ignore its staleness, Barbara tried baptizing her crumb cake, but it fell apart. She told me Brian was like a dog lapping up water from a dish. "He was all over the place. I kept saying, 'Make an ampersand, make an ampersand for fuck's sake.' It was okay, though. Kind of weird. We let Joel watch."

I imagined her growling, her orange breasts like plastic googly eyes glued to a cardboard plain where dolphins roamed, while Joel sat in the corner, his breath heavy. Brian did not know what an ampersand was because his knowledge fell only with how to fix things.

After a nor'easter last winter, a partially restored whaleship from a nearby living history maritime museum had banked on our jetty. Using found timber, Brian made a seahorse swing that was as breathtaking as it was structurally sound. Some New York fashion magazine editor spotted the swing in conch.'s Memorial Day sale and we later found it cloned on Etsy, selling for quadruple its initial cost. Brian was born too dumb to care about artistic rights. He had forgotten he even knurled the seahorse in the first place, just as he forgot how to make Barbara cum.

When anyone talked about the mainland like it was somewhere impossible to return to, I'd go especially silent. My reservations were well-plotted personality points implemented to instill a sense of wonder. I was gradually laying the foundation for a great escape. No, a retirement in the Cape was not Nancy Ballister's final act. Not if rustic lighting continued to over perform in the craft marketplace. From the same whaling wreckage others had scuttled, I found my ticket in the form of a lantern hidden underneath a heap of rope.

Our boutiques were already inflated with rope crafts, so no one had bothered with it. It wasn't until I inspected the lantern at home that I realized how valuable this treasure was. Copper and tin housing orbited a handmade glass orb, perfectly blown without air bubbles. The encased candle within was the original, made from a paraffin and spermaceti blend. Even the hinge was intact. All I had to do was glue in a burn pot, a basin for a solution of Dawn, vanilla extract, and clementine skins.

My masterpiece was to make its big debut next summer as part of the first holiday displays. Front and center would be my deconstructed aromatic lanterns that recalled a time when beasts existed to be hunted. They'd all 'ooh' and 'aah,' turning my genius in their hands and in their heads. *Nan, I knew you were creative but not this creative. Your secret gift was just hiding in there all this time. Look at you.* I would buy Barbara the Botox she always talked about. I'd get Ned that bus ticket to see his girlfriends so he wouldn't have to deal with us old biddies anymore. I'd free everyone here.

At lunch, the crumb cake was trying to sneak back up my throat on a gush of Snapple, now all a restless slough within me. Stay down, stay down, I told it. It was the day when they cut down what was left of the effigy and the food trucks emptied what was left of their season's bounty. This year they had special bluefin on a bed of pineapple salsa. I thought it tasted like crushed Advil but no one believed me. People walked around with tiny paper cups brimming with fried oysters, pickled oysters, double repacked oysters capped with mustard and oysters served raw on the half shell.

Every autumn, high winds and cooler temperatures trapped a bevy of marine life, keeping all kinds of stunned fish and crustaceans in our cove to be scooped up. There was a painting in the library of the original indigenous population taking advantage of this exact weather pattern, their nets bursting with cod. Somebody in an ambiguous mollusk costume roved the crowd. We watched him dance, chewing only on our ginger beers. Barbara said she had had her fill of swallowing slimy things whole last night. The mollusk mascot stopped to pose with the mayor, who was wearing two windbreakers at once. There was no one photographing them.

Mrs. DiStefano was making me nervous. She had ventured far too close to the railing of the bridge and curled her toes around the first rung. I thought of the ghost mopeds all stuck in amber down there. I recalled the pond behind my old house. How the geese made it seem like we inherited a farm, before they turned our swimming pool into their swamp. Off the springboard, green water clapping at my ribs. Chlorine mixing with gin in my stomach. Something brushing against my feet and wondering how a sea monster had made its way into a neighborhood pool. Being yelled at for tracking water on the new hickory kitchen floor before spending the night in our guest room. Swallowing grocery store sushi whole like a shot after work instead of going home. Going home to find a 'Nancy's Farm' sign, hand carved and displayed above our fireplace. Sorry, I'm sorry for the way I acted, that wasn't me and that wasn't us. The rest slipped away. A locked room that I could only wander from.

People at the festival tried balancing their plates on a stack of milk crates used to transport chowder broth bags. The chaperones carried these like sleeping babies with the bulged corners resting on their shoulders. Some of the sacks had been punctured and their resulting trails needed to be chased away with a hose. The mollusk mascot stood still, a fabric smile with a basketball sized pearl for a heart, watching Mrs. DiStefano inches from toppling over into the canal. It waved at me, a slow wave as if it wasn't sure it recognized me from afar. Barbara was still talking about Brian's cunnilingus technique, letting the diluted chowder broth reach her open-toed sandals. She always said she wasn't complaining whenever she was complaining.

Then I saw a cloak floating through the alabaster torrent without leaving a trail. The bog witch. She swerved in between chained mopeds. Though her face was obscured, I could make out a scowl. The jagged Chiclets in her mouth. The chaperones noticed her next. They took out their phones, but they were unlike any phones I had seen. They were made from glass. As the bog witch slid by me I could hear her hissing. A spell. Fruit snacks on her breath. She was clasping something and I knew when she revealed it that we would be in danger. Luggage I bought my son for Christmas stacked on the tiny dorm room bed. A roommate with two dead parents. Embarrassed hugs. I thought about tackling the bog witch, stabbing her in the heart with an oyster knife. But I was paralyzed where I stood.

The witch neared where the chowder bags had been stored. She climbed onto the pallet. With tiny white fists she pulled her hood down, and that was when we saw what it was. Its face was not that of a hag, but a young boy. Barbara dropped her spoon, splattering cream and celery. One by one we turned our attention to the kid. All of us, intoxicated with fresh seafood, ready for death. Helping with art homework at the kitchen table. A pit where my husband refinished its surface and cut away the crayon wax. Birthday present Saab split by a crater where our son smacked the guy in the crosswalk. You shouldn't have spoiled him with that car. With that phone. Barbara's minivan. "Barbara, when's the last time you even drove a car?"

The kid raised his hand. He had the mayor's bullhorn. A murmur went through the crowd and fell silent. The kid acknowledged them with a nod. In the full light of day, he looked made from wet straw. A siren could be heard, maybe five or ten blocks away. The kid raised the bullhorn, pressed the button and began to speak.

"Look down at your hands you fuckin' turds! Look how veiny they are," the kid said, trailed by the bullhorn's coughing feedback. His mullet chased the breeze. "Focus on them. Your hands let you invent your own lives and have trapped you here like fog. Those hands signed your papers. Remember?

But you're free now. You've been free. Run. Go out those gates. Run to the sea! Go!" He lisped through bare gums. He was maybe laughing a little. There were no gates. Just the cement and the chaperones now latching a new tent to sell crabs from. The mascot spinning in circles.

He looked back down at us with the same chin I had when I saw the pesticide signs in our driveway, knowing my husband had killed the geese. It made my sinuses sting when I thought about this and Barbara started cackling like she forced herself to understand a joke. From the town center's intersection, a pack of black SUVs tore in, lights spitting from their muzzles. Out of each door came police unlike the whistle blowing groundhogs who normally patrolled our town. Guns hung from their belts next to black flashlights. The radios on their shoulders spoke in voices of people from the past.

"Remember, try to remember under your—" but an old hand reached up and stole away the megaphone and the kid was then scooped off the milk crate, disappearing into the clutches of a red-haired woman with a face that appeared puffy from years of crying. "Your lighthouse, your lighthouse," he screamed, looking directly at me. "Your missing things are behind the lighthouse. You can go there. I've seen it."

Our initial shock devolved to laughter. The bog witch was gone with the sad red-haired woman. The crab men shrugged and made jokes with their little cigarettes just barely balancing on their lips. *Get your fresh waffle cone crab meat sundaes. Get 'em before they're warm.* They presented to us their overfed crustaceans, claws drooping beneath armored bellies. Regarding us with black bulbs that were neither dead or asleep. The ice under the bins melted into larger tributaries that collected by a storm drain.

"Well, I guess we found our sorceress," Barbara said, but her own laugh was metallic. Our voices shook when we tried to use them. We carried our fried oyster cartons as props. Everyone buried themselves back into the festival, sucking juices through the plastic limbs, and the familiarity was not a comfort this time.

In the morning, the sun had cooked death itself into any fallen leaves. The front page of the Chatham Gazette read TIME TRAVELING SORCERESS FINALLY CAUGHT BEFORE NEARLY SPOILING 6TH ANNUAL OYSTER FESTIVAL. Barbara told me she was going to papier-mâché the article directly onto a globe for her newest idea, a line of kid-chic science projects. She had stolen a cue ball from the Beachcomber Bar & Grille. That was going to be Pluto. Its actual lightness as a celestial body would be ironic in the heaviness of the resin. A long-awaited sequel to her yarn river system and baking soda volcano that erupted onto an unsuspecting gingerbread town. Now Barbara pined for dwarf starfish to wash up so she could super glue them into her milky way.

It would be the youthful thing to do. To follow the warning of a fake bog witch that had most likely been living off ladybugs and moss in the woods. There was something very Nancy Drewian about all of it. We'd stay safely far away from the lighthouse but get just close enough where we could brag forever at cocktail receptions. The afternoon had barely broken, so our excursion would conclude long before dark while it was still safe. We'd make a day of it, pack a picnic, and even stop at Brian's house to pick him up. He'd love nothing more than to protect two ladies on a dangerous voyage into the unknown, into the world of accursed nautical landmarks. It would intensify the survivor sex that he and Barb would get into afterward.

We had both received Vineyard Vines sweatshirts as gifts from tourists last year, which were now fixed around our waists in case it got cold. I sharpened a letter opener on the curb outside Barbara's house and snuck the weapon into a fanny pack.

We found Brian in his driveway, swirling wax on his Camaro. His home was a brick, single-floored ranch. Here one could see him watching sports on TV at night. Sometimes Barbara or someone who looked like her would be on the couch beside him, glowing in the blue light and knitting things that would never be finished. We told him about the boy witch and how it had stolen the mayor's bullhorn. He didn't care or trouble himself enough to make anything of it.

We told Brian we were going past the lighthouse. "You can come, but it's going to be dangerous," Barbara said. This was Barbara talk for something else. Brian's brows joined in the middle. I never noticed he had so many threads of white in his beard, or how his denim jacket bloated in the shoulders. At the announcement of our mission, Brian did not seem scared but rather resigned to something that lived either inside his home, the Camaro, or his giant jacket.

"You go," he told us. "You go." I thought Barbara was going to kneel and kiss his mouth. Instead, she patted him on the head like a dog. "I'll need some lunch," he said and left us. We could see then, under where his rag had been, the silver under the Camaro's paint showing, and tires flecked by rot.

Neither Barbara nor I had ever been near enough to the silo where it wasn't a blur. The cove it presided over had lost its drawl and the receded tide left kelp at its base. Grape producing vines climbed the seaweed skirt. We could see what wounds punctured its metal skin. I could swear I heard bees thrumming.

We forged on down the coast. We saw a sandal with a torn thong on a volcanic looking rock. There were no human footprints this far out. I found oyster crackers in my pocket, but the humidity had somehow gotten through the plastic. Perhaps it would be my last chance of eating before having to forage for yams.

"I don't know if this is the time to tell you, but that feeling I've been getting, of someone watching me," Barbara said. "It's happening right now."

"You're imagining things. Let's just keep pushing forward. I mean, we're already this far." Retracing back toward the silo would mean giving up. Ahead there was a swath of forest. Splotchy, oozing olive trails just how I'd seen hanging in our galleries. To reach it we trampled up to our shins in mud that sucked at our boots. Horseflies hopped across its surface, picking around shells and the remains of whatever animals were unlucky in their own crossing.

"Don't get pulled in," Barbara said. "I'm not strong enough to get you out." She nervously carved at her fingernails, spitting the slivers out like sunflower seeds. When we turned to mark our distance, the silo was once again a smudge. Here we found ourselves, at long last, reaching the forest, a palace constructed from the same vines that suffocated the silo. Except these vines were angry. They tangled into themselves, giving an appearance of unkempt fur. Guarding its borders were signs that screamed PRIVATE PROPERTY, forcing both of us to question once more if we should turn around. It must've been about two pm, which meant the daily tapestry weaving class would just be opening. Our mud imprints were intact and retraceable. We could surrender. Nancy Drew surrendered sometimes. She had homework. She had a family.

But we didn't. We kept on into a dense mountain laurel jungle. Its sandy floor became dirt and then leaves until we were in a thicket with birds and shade and things I hadn't seen in years. The forest smelled like a spatula left on a burner inside the apartment of a very lonely person who made forts out of poorly cleaned jars of Ragu. The property markers dissipated too, putting us truly in the wilds, a place without plastic or the invention of written language. I could feel seeds and briars latching themselves to me, desperate to get anywhere else. We were careful not to step in the many droppings that littered the path. I didn't tell Barbara, but I suspected they had been left by the bog witch who wasn't actually a witch.

"Did you notice how weird Brian was acting? I don't understand men," and then Barbara stopped speaking to scream and it was in that moment I knew our inevitable murders were upon us. "Oh my God, oh my God, is that what I think it is?" Some ancient accent of hers was resurfacing, where 'god' sounded more like 'gawd.' She turned to measure my reaction. Behind her was the shape of a body, blackened to its skeleton. Leading to a mouth capable of eating car tires, were more bodies piled into a mass grave of effigies.

I told her to calm down. Getting closer, they were perfectly entwined. A classic form of space saving, one I used myself when I packed luggage. The freshest one, Albert, was on top, the only effigie not crept on by wild grapes. My son would've loved to photograph this. An art show at the community center. Black and white photography of our family ignoring one another at the dinner table, my husband drinking from the hose with his shirt off and appendix scar on display. Some childish statement about desperation in suburbia, tacked into drywall.

Should we turn back? The path was paved in animal shit. A cat's paw prints, like the padded pattern I would wash away with windshield wiper fluid on my way to work each morning. My husband says the coyotes must've gotten her. They love the pond. We'll get a new one and make her an indoor pet. Being murdered wouldn't be so bad, I guess. I could spill my secret to Barbara. Telling someone about the lanterns instead of finishing them could be so much easier.

Lemon moons hung in the trees. A cat stepped into one pair of eyes, ragged and skulking off from a branch drowned in moss. It was joined by two more, and then a half dozen, before I realized the entire canopy was made of cats, their tails coiled or trailing as their own pets. Some of their collars were rusted while others were naked in their mange.

"Have you ever seen anything like this ever? In your life?" I told Barbara they must be feral. All living together out here. A smoke colored one whose belly was low and feathered, seemed to be leading us, or it could've been we were chasing him. Whether it was toward an escape or into a trap we didn't know, and I half expected at the path's end to be greeted by some Neolithic cougar queen adorned in human skulls.

Then through the trees, there was the comfort of buildings again, of pollution and mechanical bearings. No cougar waited for us on a yarn throne. On the wall facing the forest, someone had written BEWARE THE DRUMS using pudding. The S dribbled almost to the sidewalk. There was a familiar sensation of being watched. Familiar scents too. Urine, stale sweat on cheap hotel blankets that could never not be itchy. Flies with shimmering backs collecting on burnt hamburger. Grease spilled on the grass my son carved trails into with the lawnmower. Clover breath cut in the massacre. The smoke cat chirped expectantly, knowing it had shown us something important. A second cat wrapped its oily body around my leg, tightening itself into a snake that hissed possessively at Barbara.

"What is this place? Maybe we should leave it alone," I said.

"I've never seen this part of town," Barbara said, stepping over a border made from dead sidewalk. The few people in the street were all older than us, grazing with the help of walkers. Those confined to chairs had the air of something being left out to dry. Most hung their faces, cracked from their chins to their infinite foreheads. Both cats arched nervously at the sight of the walkers before skittering back into their forest.

"Who are these people?" I held my breath around them. It felt like we had fallen into a vacuum bag engorged with someone else's lint. I imagined for a moment a secret room made for all the eggs these people were laying but quickly shuddered the idea off.

We paused to greet a woman who had taken delight in our presence, lifting her claw out from layers of a shawl made out of medical gauze. Barbara crouched down beside her.

"Steven? Steven is that you, you old hound?" She said, scanning Barbara with eyes that reflected the overcast above. Her wheelchair was decorated in what appeared to be children's stickers.

"Where are we?" I asked.

"No one tells me anything. Who has time these days?" I brushed away a hunting party of ants from her arm and saw that her wrist was squeezed inside a plastic bracelet. None of the businesses looked like they had been open in several years. A sign for Sal's Ice Cream had faded into its own paint. Another for Dunver's Pizza & Surf Shop seemed to have been almost entirely eaten by time. The doors of the ice cream parlor were covered in a filmy yellow. Inside we saw trash strewn on milkshake machines. "They never open on time, sweetie," the old woman said when she saw us looking into the windows. "Are we leaving? I'll get Harlan. Have you seen Steven? I can't find the body anywhere."

Another woman sang to us from far away and the two began chattering in their own language. From the town's heart there came a chorus, one that was youthful and without gravel. It summoned us to something of a common square, presided over by a statue of a sailor whose chest was crossed by ropes. A mermaid prowled at his legs. His head was missing. Above them in the clearing was a diamond-shaped sign for Sal's Pre-Owned Volvo and European Cars.

A circle of maybe a dozen wheelchairs were gathered in the lot. They sang through oxygen tubes a song about American highways. They were situated around a girl, reading from a paperback novel with a shirtless firefighter on the cover. Something you'd find at a grocery store. Another flicked a bubblegum tongue. She was singing to a man in a reclining beach chair. The old listened intently. Several of the men could've passed for dead, sleeping under oversized baseball caps proudly displaying patches for warships.

Our presence must have caused the girl severe alarm because she had thrown her book to the ground. She wore nursing scrubs. Her hair was fixed up into a massive bun with an array of neck strands that fanned out to make her appear as if she were about to catch fire.

"Are you supposed to be here?" She looked to her man lounging on his beach chair. His goatee bore the offspring of three necks. They wore sneakers so white they burned my eyes. He asked if we were from Hyannis and if we had any ID. Cackling came from beneath one of the warship hats.

Goatee told us we were lost. He spoke slowly as if we were children. I felt his fist open on my shoulder and then start rummaging under the sweatshirt fixed around my waist.

"We got a knife," he said to the girls behind him. He continued searching, despite my protest. From my pocket, he found a license which I didn't remember getting.

"You all have come a long way, haven't you? Shan, you watch them. We'll be back," he said to the second girl. She snapped her gum and claimed his beach chair. The sound of the six o'clock news promoting a record-breaking blizzard from the living room while I fix dinner. Melting the glaze in the microwave as directed by a Pioneer Woman recipe I printed out. Two-year-old Baskin-Robbins bubblegum ice cream from the back of the freezer used as a mixer for gin. Cracked an egg with blood in the yolk. Smoke detectors screaming about the duck left in the oven. Black, black, black. "We'll help you. We're here to help you stay on track."

Where the sneakers took us was warm. The belly of a tavern or what had once been a tavern. I asked who all those people were. "They see in grey," Goatee said. "Not like you two. You still see things in full color, isn't that right?"

Fishermen watched us from photos on the walls. The draft taps were coated in the flesh and beard hair of these men, given to protect their drink. Surely in our time, Barbara and I would've caused quite a stir. We just had poor timing. Next to the photographs were paintings, crudely composed with a grotesque sense of color. One showed a sprawling wine vineyard. Another was of men armed with machine guns, pursuing a whale from a rowboat. In the third painting, dozens of cats scampered off a docked ship. Their faces were humanlike with a determination for new land. I wondered if the faces had belonged to real people.

I mouthed the words, "Barb, look at this." There was something to connect but it was up to her to find the middle. Bun Fire took us back up to the curb. She complained it was getting too dark. That there wasn't enough electricity in this part of town. The two sneakers wandered off to share a cigarette. I heard one tell the other we were trust fund residents. "Must be nice!" It is nice, I thought.

Barbara turned to me with a plan in her face. We couldn't stay here. Something terrible was going to happen. We counted to three in nods and then burst into a jog at the same time. It had been years since I jogged. My Vineyard Vines sweatshirt came loose and was gone. Snot ran salty from my nose. Our grand escape sent the wheelers into an uproar, forcing the sneakers to stop and tend to their cattle.

Their shouts fell away. We were safe. Free as needles in a hay bale of mountain laurel again. Furious at my sudden demand from it, my knee burned up to the thigh. Branches whipped any flesh not covered by clothing. The cats were incredulous now and had retreated back to the trees. Neither Barbara nor I slowed our pace until we could hear the beach again and the signs came back into view. On the reverse of the signs in three different languages, there were longer warnings. *Do you have these symptoms? Do NOT physically engage with patients. Please wear mouth protection. Foreign germs can KILL.* We ignored them and carried onward so that our backs were to PRIVATE PROPERTY again. Caught our breath and swallowed what insects were trapped in our throats.

Over the hill, it was starting to get dark. The mud we crossed was frozen solid. Bullfrogs mooed as they became trapped in it. The painters had left behind their work of the silo. This didn't surprise me, as the summer's glowing meadows had browned considerably and who would want to paint a thing so sad? When I saw their abandoned canvases, I saw only a violence of slathered markings. Handprints. Their easels were anchored by bricks, so we kicked them over. We destroyed them.

3.

It was exactly one week later when the boat came. There was no warning of its arrival. Any remaining lifeguards were on their break, as their ranks had been thinned out from the ease that shared whistles filled them with a virus. He was a fisherman. A gunner from a far-off war. Tattoos of scriptures tangling with strange desert beasts reached all the way to his knuckles. Barbara confessed her love for him almost immediately.

The gunner had found something in the sea, pulled up during a haul of bluefin. The body of Mrs. DiStefano, spat out by the canal and trapped in the cove by the same weather that gave us our bountiful seafood. The chaperones carried her, still wrapped in a net, and they would say she looked like she was sleeping but I saw her and she did not. The police came back. The ones with long flashlights instead of whistles. They stood in a circle with the gunner and laughed and tugged up their pants by the belts.

"The rest of them went back to school," Ned said. The two of us were playing rummy in the booth of a fancy tapas place, shuttered up for the winter. "Me? I'm not going back. I'm going to make some real money laying tile with my uncle." He had thrown his apron over the bridge and told me it was for the eels now. Ned told me how fond he had been of Mrs. DiStefano, but only when I asked him if he missed all the girls who left. I never imagined he would give so much credence to a silly fossil of a woman like her. "Don't worry, I left some scones in the apron pocket." I didn't know if he meant they were for the eels or Mrs. DiStefano.

"My mother once mixed up salt and sugar in her scones and both my father and I pretended not to notice. We ate every one," I said, adding to the discard pile. Ned watched the table. He was growing a beard.

"I saw her, Nan. No one should have to see their own grandmother like that." I wasn't sure what he meant by grandmother. I didn't follow how young people spoke anymore. "She was see-through, you know. The cove is merciless on a body. All those crabs the restaurants have been doping up. They got her good. They'll go for anything soft. Nose, eyes, ears. Your chin." Ned put his head down and whimpered. I think it was Ned. He could've been anyone. I rubbed circles into his hand and told him things from the cougar show reruns but whispered them in a way that was gentler.

"I have to pack," he said. Before he got up to leave, he removed something from his pocket that appeared to have been folded for a very long time. "I salvaged this from the bonfire. Think of it as a new version of yourself every day. You don't have to track your bills or worry about who's going to take care of you. You're here because someone out there really cares. Like the real kind of caring. That's a good thing. Not everyone has that," and I saw then he had given me a brochure.

We slowed in and out of hibernation. The chill made my knee act up. It was a carpeted winter sewed from forty-one-degree days. The snow melted just as soon as it streaked the dune grass. Some of the winter tourists came for discounted rates, sitting to dinner with new transfers. People I never saw before. Probably from the city. They avoided the constant wind and sleet by sheltering inside a Hibachi restaurant that served grouper sour enough to conjure almost immediate nausea. The winter visitors loved the silo. Our monument would return as black and white portraits in every gallery. Locals left. Some forever. Lee Howardson, our resident woodcarver, succumbed to the unfortunate act of cutting himself in half. The rumor was suicide, though

Lee loved generic brand tortilla chips and had most likely finished off his brain with GMOs. Something Ned would've said.

On Labor Day weekend I had visitors. They were looking for directions to the Atwood Gallery and we "just got to talking," as Capers called it. They were two tourists, an older man and a younger one who both went by Randy. They bore the same faces too. Randy Sr. said there was a third who couldn't make it because she had gotten trapped somewhere out in the Midwest, but she sent her best. I asked them if she was Randy too and they laughed. They worried about my limp. We watched an ocean from rocking chairs on an enclosed porch, enjoying the heat from propane lamps. We sat down to breakfast at Hammy's Diner where the eggs tasted like trout on account of our farm chickens living off fish feed for the winter. They took care of the bill. We purposely forgot our doggy bags. We washed our mouths out with coffee and we saw in the parking lot a seagull kill another seagull.

"Let's go to the beach. You people like the beach," I told them.

At the shore, the wind was chopping up the waves, battering any surviving sandcastles the young tourists had built, their royal subjects long buried or consumed by fleas. In their remains was a calcified starfish. Randy Jr. picked it up.

"I'll bet you could make something real nice out of this. Isn't this like gold to you people if it's got all five limbs?"

When the afternoon got too chilly we walked back to town. They had already painted a second coat to the effigy wall. Golden primer. On another building, they were touching up a mural of a sperm whale. Its smell was sticky and repeated in my brain. In the window of our newest boutique, citrine&SALT, teddy bears waited in a perfect, miniature forest made from cones of rich green construction paper. A card indicated they were hand sewn with found sea glass eyes and stuffed with mallard down, their whiskers crafted from real fisher cat pelts. A remedy for homesickness. Something about the display made me want to set fire to its forest. Free the bears before they were sold for their $80 listing price, only to be left behind, because more familiar, tried and true bears waited at home for the summering children. In the next window, a statue's head modeled pearl jewelry.

The two Randy's brought me to their hotel, to a chilly room on the fourth floor. They turned up the thermostat and I fell asleep watching new episodes on TV.

4.

"Hey, they've got Ray Liotta as Colonel Sanders now," the younger Randy said when I woke up. I had slept until dark. His chin was like my chin. We shared a long goodbye which are my favorite kind of goodbyes. Old Randy still had his sleeves rolled up and I saw on his wrist a drawing of an arrow. The kind a hunter would fire. When he saw what I had noticed he gave a brief nod to my wrist with its letter D. We hugged. The smell that came off his nape brought with it spilled nail polish on a computer keyboard. Typing my symptoms into the search bar and being confronted with a disease. One that doesn't stop attacking. I found others like me on internet forums. LindaLovesTheRedSox57: *Your brain will soften. It's less like an animal attack and more of a replacing, except it replaces you with gaps.* Scouring forums late into the night and then sneaking into bed with my husband, totally oblivious to the expiration date now given to me. I wondered if LindaLovesTheRedSox57 was dead. I wondered who else on that message board was dead. Before they left, the Randy's promised they'd be seeing more of me now that it was getting a little warmer again.

It was a good day to settle into the cafeteria. Here I found a woman whose hair bloomed like a marigold with silver at the roots. I liked that about her, though she hated the cold and made everyone suffer for it. Seated next to her was a man with work gloves trying to push tea across the table. On his lap sat a small, well-behaved dog. A spaniel, I think. The woman was chatty.

"Do you remember when we visited the colony of leopards? Did you see the stillborn Camaro?" She asked me this and the man took back the tea, taking his gloves off, putting them back on. "This is my husband," she said. "Have you met him?" The man gave me a glassy smile, though his chin was too covered with beard to know.

I dreamt of this back in my room. Here, underneath my pillow, I kept my brochure. It showed me paintings of people, walking an outdoor mall where weeds did not grow from the cuts in the sidewalk. *Dignified care for your loved ones. Only in the crown crest of Arbors: New England, can you escape together.* I cut out the pictures of the people and tacked them to the drywall beside my bed until the brochure was gone. Who could feel sorry for these people? They didn't live anywhere. These tourists that came and went, came and went.

HOT MOUNTAIN

There's good dumpster diving in Ottawa. The Nordic Isle Buffet throws out whole steamed lobsters. Farlburg Family Ford doesn't send their tire rims back to corporate to be destroyed. The Jemns Inn factory fills their dumpsters with baskets and authentic New England crafts. After the holidays I wake up early and snag any rejected candles that didn't make it to labeling. Their identity can only be surmised by color. If I had siblings I'd send these home as gifts. Jemns Inn once melted down their shrink, glass and all. When their filtration system died, everyone would know exactly how close autumn was when the wind shifted to canvass the city in mauve. Periwinkle in the summer.

It would be better to be home in Michigan with Arnie playing Call of Duty, having some beers and bringing up his old girlfriend so I could fall asleep to him talking about her. I could tell it was summer there when Arnie's new girlfriend would bring us pink lemonade with messages hidden in ice cubes.

Their house was a terrarium with its fudge climate and carpet moss. I could tell it was summer there when Grandma Heather's leg veins resurfaced. She was the adopted kind of grandma that came built-in with the couch. Forever watching Arnie's floating rifle blow up oil drums, to feel consumed by such AWESOME graphics. Inside of afternoons, she would sing to us about how the whole house had secret oak flooring and that it was beautiful.

We knew it was spring when the smell of jizz was in the air. "Pyrus calleryana trees do this when they bloom," Arnie would say. He combated them by starting a reiki tree removal business. Before this we used to steal chainsaws, remove the belt and use them as props in his garage/haunted house. $10 leading up to Halloween, $5 November 1st through the 8th. Just a bunch of people paying to hang out near old paint cans, pretending to be someone else.

"I tap into the life energy in these things and bam—I let 'em have it. Have what? You don't want to know, man." His palms becoming flattened oyster tongues. Always drifting. Arnie made enough money to buy a batch of yard signs. *Reiki Tree Removal—Call Arnie.*

"You don't wanna know how many jizz trees I've slaughtered. I deserve this." This was what he told me after sleeping with other women and ignoring Grandma Heather's hospital bills. I went with him to buy a used Honda that had only 32,000 miles on it. This number was written on its windshield in glass chalk. On the back panel it still faintly read *Congrats FHS Seniors, Go Wildlions.* I helped him scrape that off, and I helped him hold cardboard in the sun to better light the dong pics he sent out. His Publishers Clearing House mailers.

Arnie's girlfriend divorced him by writing a message on the tub wall in her hair. Grandma Heather was finally eaten by the couch. When they tore up the carpet, it was only planks of little mites underneath. After that, Arnie was too depressed to move. But I wasn't. Putting on his mask simply involved lining up the mouth slit, tucking my own hair behind the band, and changing the phone number on all his yard signs.

To throw out your past is even easier. Upon getting rich by charming away unwanted nut-bearers/car-denters using only my mind, I stuffed my old flannels into garbage bags. Five years of winter spreading apart the seams to reveal the tentacle arms with their button suckers. I drove Arnie's car to the Goodwill bin and pushed all those winters into the mouth.

You can carve a key like a shank. Sometimes it's already unlocked. Either way, your clothes will hunt their way back to you. Listen to the woolen bloodhounds, as Grandma Heather would say. Even when they're scratching and barking at your door, no one says you have to hear them.

To dive deeper is all fish skeletons swimming in perfect muck or W9 forms shredded into snow. It's Big Mac shells where strange mollusks have, at long last, found a home. But I'm rich enough to drink coffee indoors now and can point out the people who wear my hand-me-downs as all new younger brothers and sisters. You really only miss the chlorine when its spirit's annual visits stop. Everything will seem strangely fresh. Then I'll come back up.

Stories Contained in This Collection Have Previously Appeared In

Bridge Eight Press

Five Quarterly

FIVE:2:ONE Magazine

formercactus

Ghost City Review

Joyland Magazine

Love on the Road 2013 (Malinki Press)

OCCULUM

Owl Canyon Press

SAND Journal

Sediments Literary-Arts Journal

Sporklet

The Head & the Hand Press, Breadbox Chapbook Series

The Tishman Review

X-R-A-Y Literary Magazine

Seafoam Green is based on the story *Seafoam Green*
by Aqua Drakes and Travis Dahlke

Out to Lunch Records

Out to Lunch Records seeks to challenge, innovate, and explore new ways of creating and engaging on a musical and extra-musical level. All things avant, absurd, and oppositional are welcomed. The spirit of Dada and DIY are present and encouraged. Operating as a creative collective, Out to Lunch is not a genre or aesthetic specific music label, and that will be reflected in our output and artists alike. Out to Lunch Records was formed out of a natural progression of collaborations and friendships in and around the Boston music scene, arising as a creative solution to a vastly changing musical landscape. The Lunch Break Zine serves as the literary arm of the label, providing a platform for writers, poets, and visual artists to share their work.

Visit their website at outtolunchrecords.com.

The Soundtrack

Always a work in progress, FiFac (Jeff Dragan) is a Connecticut based producer with a focus on texture. Crystalline drone and aggressive variants of ambient using various synthesizers, effects, and samplers.

Find him via Instagram @jeffdragan.

The Illustrator

John Shields is a New England based illustrator and videographer, working across a variety of mediums, including digital, ink, and paint. He has created published work for advertising, graphic novellas, product packaging and has been featured in galleries and event posters. John holds a degree in Digital Art & Multimedia from MxCC in Middletown, CT. He is currently working on a full-length comic about Civil War reenactors.

Find him via Instagram @db.john.

The Author

Travis Dahlke is the author of *Hollow as Legs* (Otherwhere Press). His fiction has appeared in Joyland Magazine, Outlook Springs, No Contact, and The Longleaf Review, among other literary journals and collections. His novella, *Milkshake* is forthcoming from Long Day Press in March 2022. He lives in Middletown, Connecticut.

Visit his website at travis-dahlke.com.

ISBN 978-0-578-30488-5

9 780578 304885